THE DANCE MASTER

THE DANCE MASTER

Peter Turnbull

This first world edition published in Great Britain 2004 by
SEVERN HOUSE PUBLISHERS LTD of
9–15 High Street, Sutton, Surrey SM1 1DF.
This first world edition published in the USA 2004 by
SEVERN HOUSE PUBLISHERS INC of
595 Madison Avenue, New York, N.Y. 10022.

British Library Cataloguing in Publication Data

Turnbull, Peter, 1950-
  The dance master
  1. Hennessey, George (Fictitious character) - Fiction
  2. Yellich, Somerled (Fictitious character) - Fiction
  3. Police - England - Yorkshire - Fiction
  4. Detective and mystery stories
  I. Title
  823.9'14 [F]

  ISBN 0-7278-6080-1

Typeset by Palimpsest Book Production Ltd.,
Polmont, Stirlingshire, Scotland.
Printed and bound in Great Britain by
MPG Books Ltd., Bodmin, Cornwall.

One

in which the number twelve assumes a significance.

The flats had always been a bad building. Not high as flats go, a mere twelve storeys, because this was the city of York, where no building was allowed to over-shadow the Minster. Now twelve years old, a year for each storey, ground to the eleventh, they had seen twelve summers and were in the lag end of their twelfth winter, and they had always been a bad building. The design was bad, bad for the north of England, with wind and rain, lots of rain, but the design had been approved 'because it worked in southern France' was the meek and much publi-cized and much ridiculed retort. In the north of England the design, which worked in southern France, allowed the building to become black with damp, rapidly so. And the design which worked so well in southern France was unable to keep out the slicing, biting east wind of a Yorkshire winter. The flats were damp and draughty, cold and impos-sible to heat, and still only twelve years old; with a design life of in excess of one hundred years. The construction of the flats had been marred by one ill event after another, particularly deaths. In all, four workmen had died during the construction, all accidentally, none in suspicious circumstances, not linked, save for the fact that they had

1

all died on the same site, an Englishman, an Irishman, a Scotsman and a Welshman . . . like the first line of a juvenile joke. There were in addition eight serious accidents: twelve accidents all told. Particularly tragic was the death of the twelve-year-old boy who, along with his mates, had found the site an irresistible adventure playground and fallen to his death from the scaffolding at the top floor. Again, the figure twelve was associated with the flats. The construction of the building hadn't been smooth. It had been a construction achieved in fits and starts and the figure twelve occurred yet again . . . the strike which lasted for twelve weeks, an economic recession which forced the company to lay off the workforce for twelve months. The flats, officially Cambridge House, were named solely to give the building an air of prestige, there being no connection at all with the city of Cambridge or the illustrious university therein, on Askham Road, YO23. Commissioned as high-amenity flats for the most socially responsible of the city's council-dwelling families and with a higher rent, Cambridge House rapidly deteriorated as the tenants refused to live there, demanding dry, heatable accommodation for themselves and their children. The reputation of the flats spread and the 'desirable' tenants, the people whom the council had wanted to place in their new flagship medium-rise housing block, refused to accept accommodation there. Within two years of it being completed, Cambridge House had become a dumping ground for the antisocial families of the city, the chronically unemployed and unemployable, the criminals, the homeless, who had no say in where they were housed. 'It's Cambridge House or the street, take it or leave it,' and with no political weight to call on, such people, often young, would 'take it'. The flats became a locus for addiction, with rusty hypodermics in the staircases; the lifts, which rarely worked, began to give off the permanent stench of stale, and often not so stale, urine, and the shifting population began to average one murder every twelve months. Always a 'domestic', victim and perpetrator often living with each other, or known to each other in some way, always the result of a sudden explosion of violence often drink or drug induced, never gangland, never premeditated, just low life, about as low as life can get in the graceful city of York. There was widely believed to be a curse on the building and indeed a local historian of no mean repute offered the story to the press of the tale of Samantha Hopkins, who was convicted of witchcraft in the early seventeenth century and who was burned at the stake on the very spot on which Cambridge House was later to be built. Before the torches were applied to the kindling, she cursed the spot upon which she was to die and her lips were observed to move as if in cursing, for twelve minutes, before she succumbed to the flames. Once the story of Samantha Hopkins' curse had been printed and picked up and amplified by the local television stations, it became even more difficult to house people in Cambridge House and, one by one, the individual flats were closed and sheets of metal were placed over the entrance doors and bolted in place. Yet even that would not keep out the squatters or the down-and-outs who 'skippered' in the empty flats, sleeping on the floor softened with newsprint after escaping from reality with the aid of a tin of liquid brass polish. That was Cambridge House in the February of the year in which the bones were found.

Twelve of them.

Matthew Hopkins lived on the top floor of Cambridge House. He was a young man, just twenty-four years of age, and he lived in the generous space of a four-roomed flat which had been designed for use of a nuclear family, but since no one would live in the flats, the Council Housing Department had been obliged to offer homeless

Matthew Hopkins a large flat to himself. It was by then not at all unusual for the Housing Department to allocate family accommodation in Cambridge House to the single homeless. Matthew Hopkins was not a man of learning and it was to be some years hence before he discovered his namesake to have been the infamous 'Witchfinder General'. Nor did he know of the story of his namesake Samantha Hopkins and her curse, and so was not able to ponder upon the resilience of the English language, which allowed a name to survive intact from medieval times to the twenty-first century. He was, in fact, a desperate live-for-the-day, long-term heroin addict who led a feral-like existence, sallying forth from his cold and lonely flat to beg or looking for things to steal or to acquire, people, vulnerable people, like the elderly, to rob for a few pounds, sometimes even only a few coins, picking up tin cans which he could sell for a penny each to the recycling plant, until he had enough money for a 'fix'. He was slight, drawn, deathly pale, insufficiently clad for the winter and, one morning in February, he left his flat and stepped out on to the landing, which was exposed to the elements, intending to walk to the lift shaft and thence into the city to begin the day begging near the Minster, when he saw the plastic bag. It was not a bin liner used to collect domestic refuse – that he would have ignored. Probably. It was a bag with the name of a shop upon the side, and it looked new, as if it had been placed there very, very recently, put down and forgotten, and abandoned. Matthew Hopkins pounced on it, lusted after it, wrenching it open, and then withdrew, as if jolted by a charge of electricity. For the bag did not contain the money he had dreamed of finding, nor valuables he could unload to shady dealers in the city, but bones. He closed the bag and thought. He didn't like the police, they didn't like him, but he wasn't wanted for anything. There were no outstanding warrants against him . . . and for this . . . for this . . . there might be a reward. If nothing else, the papers or the television might pay for his story. It would be worth a fix at least because they were not just bones . . . they were human bones. The skull said so. He ran to the lift, took it to the ground floor, ran to the phone box which stood in the forecourt of Cambridge House and dialled three nines.

Little went unseen at Cambridge House and a known smackhead running to the phone box attracted the attention of the one or two people who just happened to be looking out of their front-facing windows as Matthew Hopkins darted across the forecourt. And the news spread rapidly, by word of mouth, by banging on the dividing wall between flats, and when Matthew Hopkins had finished his breathless description of his find to the police phone operator and had promised to wait by the phone, he replaced the receiver and turned to see many faces staring at him from windows on all the twelve floors of the block of flats. It was something he had not anticipated and he knew that suspicion would be aroused when the police vehicle came. He was confident he could weather it. He wasn't informing on anyone. If he didn't report the bones, someone else would. Simple as that, and he only did it for the reward. There had to be a reward. He leaned back against the phone box, a new clear Perspex box of the favoured EEC design, sheltering from the wind which blew keenly about the court. He glanced up. The sky was overcast. It would, he thought, rain later. That would limit his choices that day. When the rain hit the deck he needed shelter, and from sheltered places, folk of his ilk get rapidly moved on by the police, or shop security people in their uniforms. On that day, though, he could get through if there was a reward . . . if . . . if . . . if.

The patrol turned off Askham Road and into the forecourt of Cambridge House. Seeing it, Matthew Hopkins raised a hand and walked towards it. He couldn't resist glancing at the flats and saw that the number of people now gazing at him and the police constables had doubled, tripled even. But that was Cambridge House. The residents were unemployed and a police vehicle turning into the forecourt was what amounted to a 'main event' of the day. Hopkins identified himself to the two officers and repeated the details of his find. The three men then walked back into Cambridge House itself and Hopkins pressed the 'call' button beside the lift shaft. The metal doors rumbled slowly open – the lift was clearly already at the ground floor – and a strong smell of urine emerged, causing the younger constable to step back, making a groaning sound.

'I knew you were going to smell that,' the other constable grinned.

'Well, thanks for the warning.'

'Cambridge House,' the second constable said, stepping into the lift. 'You'll come here plenty of times, you may as well get used to it.'

Hopkins and the first, the younger, constable followed the second, more experienced, constable into the lift. The second constable pressed the 11 button on the chrome panel. Hopkins stood in the corner of the lift. The police had taken over now. It was by then their show, and he well knew his place when in the company of police officers. The lift rose steadily, but slowly, shifting gently from side to side as it did so. It was not the speedy, smooth ride of lifts in office blocks or department stores which fill the users with confidence as their feet are pressed to the floor, but rather an unnerving ride during which none of the three spoke, because, Hopkins thought, the ride induced the feeling that if the lift became stuck, it would not be unexpected. There was a distinct sense of relief felt by all three men when the lift halted at the top floor,

6

followed by a wait of a few seconds before the doors rumbled open, allowing the east wind to claw their faces, but it was fresh air, very fresh and distinctly and definitely preferable to the stale air within the metal box that was the lift in Cambridge House.

'This way.' Hopkins led the officers along the exposed outside walkway, doors of the flats to his left, a balcony to his right, about three feet high, which offered a view of the expanse of housing and beyond that the Vale of York, at that point a vista of drab greys and browns and just a little green. 'There.' He pointed to the bag which still stood where he had left it.

'Which is your flat, Matthew?' The senior constable spoke with a solid Yorkshire accent of quiet authority.

'The door after the bag.'

'Beyond the bag,' the younger constable growled and as he did so Hopkins noticed the senior officer throwing him a disapproving glance. He evidently felt it not an appropriate moment to correct the grammar of a helpful member of the public.

'The bag wasn't here last night, you say, Matthew?'

'No, sir . . .' Hopkins added 'sir' involuntarily. Too often he'd been nervously rescuing what he could at the charge bar. 'I'm behaving myself, aren't I, sir . . . ?'

The constable picked up on the use of the word 'sir'. 'Known to us, are you, Matthew?'

'Little things. Nothing in the pipeline . . . that's why I called you. If I knew you were looking for me, I wouldn't have called you.'

'You mean you've been getting away with it.' The senior constable smiled as they approached the bag. 'We'll do a check anyway. What's your date of birth?' He took his notepad out and scribbled Hopkins' date of birth as Hopkins dictated it. 'So you looked in the bag?'

'Yes . . . it was just sitting there as I left my flat . . .

not a refuse bag . . . see for yourself, like a bag from a big shop. I thought there'd be some treasure in it.'

'Treasure?'

'Something I could use, something I could sell.'

'Otherwise known as theft by finding, but that wouldn't bother you, would it, Matthew?'

Hopkins shrugged.

'So . . .' The senior constable kneeled and pulled the bag open using his pen. 'I see.' He turned to the junior constable. 'Want a look?'

'No, thanks.' The junior constable glanced out over the roof tops of the Vale beyond.

Hopkins, who had known police officers from his very early days and had learned how to 'read' them, thought the junior constable not only new to police work, but ill-suited as well. He thought him the sort of man who would leave after a brief period and take up something gentler, primary-school teaching for instance, wherein he could explain the difference between 'after' and 'beyond'.

'Well –' the senior constable stood – 'I see what you mean, Matthew. They look real. The skull . . . the bones . . . not recent though, no flesh at all.' He grabbed his radio, which was attached to his collar, and reported suspicious human remains, gave the location and asked for CID and crime scene examiners. He listened as his request was acknowledged and then switched the radio to receive. 'You didn't see or hear anything last night, Matthew?'

'About the bag? No. I was out most of the time . . . I have a habit . . . but you won't find anything on me or in my drum.'

'I believe you, Matthew.' Hopkins could see that the officer saw him as an end user, harmless, pathetic, very sad. 'I thought there might be a reward.'

'I see. Not as public-spirited as I thought. Eye for the main chance, eh?'

'I had nothing to lose.'

'And everything to gain. Well, there might be . . . depends who he or she is. Then again, there may not be.'

'Will the newspapers pay?'

'They may.' The constable saw Hopkins' eyes brighten with expectation. 'Right now, you just go back in your flat and wait there . . . My boss will want to talk to you.'

'Wait . . .' Hopkins wailed. 'I can't . . . I should be on the town now . . . I have a habit.'

'Get into your flat!'

George Hennessey peered into the plastic bag. They were, he saw, indeed bones. 'Well –' he stood – 'I dare say the skull makes them human. Found by . . . ?'

'The young fella who lives here, sir.' The constable pointed towards Matthew Hopkins' flat. 'I don't think he will be of much use to you though.'

'Oh?'

'Well, he claims to have heard nothing in respect of the bag. He's a heroin addict . . . known to us for theft in the main . . . and he told me he was well out of his skull last night.'

Hennessey glanced at the constable. 'Well out of his skull?'

'Comatose with heroin . . . having injected himself.'

'Ah.' Hennessey screwed his trilby down tighter on his head as a gust of wind threatened to relieve him of it. He read the logo on the bag. 'Whitelands.'

'Don't know it, sir.'

'Neither do I.' Hennessey glanced at the bag. It was a dark-green colour, quite restful on the eyes, he found, and the legend 'Whitelands' was printed in black. The two colours seemed to go well together. 'A bit classy,' he said.

'Classy, sir?'

'Yes . . . sort of haughty . . . a bit nose in the air. What's that expression? Upmarket . . .'

'You think so, sir?'

'Well, hone your powers of observation, Constable. I don't think your mate will.' Hennessey glanced along the walkway. The junior constable had wandered to the end of the walkway and had appointed himself sentinel. 'I get the impression that the bones were too much for him . . . he's found himself a job well away from the locus. So, why do I say "classy"?'

'Can't think, sir. It's a plastic bag . . . you'd get the same from any supermarket.'

'Would you?'

'Well, wouldn't you, sir?'

Hennessey smiled. He knew the constable, Clark by name, a cheery 29-year-old, married with a newborn son, developing a certain cynicism, which all police officers have to a greater or lesser extent. But a man with a future in the police unlike, Hennessey thought, unlike his younger colleague, whom he also knew, Constable Thackery by name, who still lived with his mother and seemed to shy away from everything he encountered. He was not the most inspired appointment to the police. 'No,' he said, 'you wouldn't. It has a reinforced handle . . . it's a bit posh . . . the plastic is thicker . . . heavier grade . . . it won't tear very easily . . . and the colours, a bit reserved, don't you think? Not the loud, gaudy colours you associate with the cut-price supermarkets . . . all yellows and reds. Black on dark green . . . it doesn't shout, "Look at me!" does it?'

'Well, no . . . since you put it like that and yes, I see what you mean, sir . . . upmarket, as you say.'

'But life being life, I will doubtless be proved wrong.' He turned as his eye was caught by movement to his left.

He saw Constable Thackery step back and allow the passage of the crime scene examiners, carrying cameras and fingerprint-lifting equipment. They approached Hennessey with polite 'Good mornings', to which Hennessey responded, equally politely, and then said, 'The bag.'

'Just the bag, sir?'

'Just the bag. Not a very large scene of crime, as scenes of crime go . . . and quite neat too. If you could photograph the bag as it is and the contents as they are.'

'What are the contents, sir?'

'Bones, as you will see.'

'Oh.' The examiner made ready his camera. 'Bones . . . dem bones dem bones . . .'

'Quite apt in this case.' Hennessey stood back to allow the examiner a clear field of vision for the photographs. 'Not a shred of flesh on them. Not that I can see.'

'Sure they're human?' The examiner smiled. 'Anatomically correct skeletons made of resin and used in schools of medicine in universities have been known to start murder inquiries. They become broken or damaged in some way and so are unfit for teaching purposes and get thrown out with the rubbish, end up on a tip, and lo and behold, a major inquiry.' The examiner pointed his camera at the plastic bag.

'Well –' Hennessey shut his eyes as protection against the flash – 'they seem human to me . . . but a resin skeleton would be quite a pleasing outcome. Frankly, I could do with wrapping this one up quickly.'

The crime scene examiner, asking his colleague to hold the camera, snapped on a pair of latex gloves and knelt before the bag. He opened it gingerly, using, as Constable Clark had done, a pen to separate the two rims of the bag. 'I see,' he said. He stood as his colleague proffered him the camera. 'It's not my place to make the diagnosis, Chief

Inspector, but I don't think you'll wrap this one up as quickly as you'd like.'

'No . . . ? Would you be saying that because there are no small metal eyelets at the end of the bones, which would be the case if they were resin?'

The examiner paused and forced a smile. 'I'll just take the photographs, sir.'

'I'd be obliged.' Hennessey returned the smile. 'Then take each item of bone out, place it on plastic sheets alongside the bag.'

'Yes, sir.'

'Photograph them.'

'Yes, sir.'

'Then take them and the bag back to Wetherby . . . lift any latents that might be there.'

'Yes, sir.'

Hennessey turned to Constable Clark. 'Radio in, please, we need more constables and ask DS Yellich to get his tail down here.'

'Yes, sir.'

'If there isn't a sergeant, you'll be acting sergeant.'

'Yes, sir. Thank you, sir.'

'Organize the constables . . . knock on every door in this block of flats . . . a thorough house-to-house. If any person has information or saw anything, the constable is not to take the statement, but to note the flat number and name of the person and provide myself or DS Yellich with that information. Either he or I will interview the person concerned.'

'Very good, sir.' PC Clark gripped his radio and pressed the 'send' button.

TUESDAY, 10.30 HOURS – 12.00 HOURS

Louise D'Acre looked at the skeletal remains, twelve items in all. They were arrayed on a stainless-steel dissecting table in the pathology laboratory of the York District Hospital. 'I'd like to ask for a second opinion.' She turned to where DCI Hennessey stood against the wall, keeping a deferential distance from the dissecting table. 'But I think you have the remains of two people here.'

'Two?'

'I think two, possibly three. The skull is male, the bones are smaller than I would expect them to be if they were part of the same body. The bones appear to be female. It's very difficult to sex bones . . . in fact it is pretty well impossible.' Dr D'Acre, a slender woman in her forties, she kept her hair cut short, dark with a hint of grey, and the only make-up she allowed herself was a trace of lipstick, and even that was of the palest hue. Hennessey thought her to be a woman who knew the advantage of graceful ageing. 'We can sex a skull, and a ribcage and a pelvis . . . but bones . . . very difficult . . . their size is the best indication. If they are large they are male, possibly, if they are smaller, they are female, possibly.' She looked again at the bones. 'But small, finely built men will have bones of the size of female bones.'

'I see.'

'I won't be drawn and I would like a second opinion . . . but we have two left clavicles – collarbones – which are small, they seem adult . . . right.' Dr D'Acre patted the table with her latex-gloved hand and smiled at Hennessey. It was something she rarely did, but had turned away again before Hennessey could recover from his surprise and return the smile. 'Let's stop complaining. Let's see what this skull and those bones can tell us . . . and that will be quite a lot. Age for one thing. We have a femur . . . and I note the epiphyseal union is complete . . . which takes place about sixteen years of age, so this person in life had achieved that age, but there is no indication of any degenerative disease which I would associate with ageing, so the impression is that this femur came from a young adult. The sternal clavicles also both show signs of epiphyseal union and that occurs about the ages of between twenty-one and twenty-seven in females . . . a little later in males, which gives a minimum and a maximum range . . . assuming of course . . . that these twelve bits didn't come from twelve different persons.'

Hennessey groaned.

'That possibility didn't occur to you Detective Chief Inspector?' Dr D'Acre glanced at him but did not smile.

'Confess it didn't,' Hennessey replied. 'When I saw them, I thought: One person . . . we'll find the rest of him or her somewhere else.'

'I'm afraid it's a possibility you can't discount. DNA testing will confirm it though, one way or the other.' She returned her attention to the bones. 'The remaining bones appear to be metacarpals . . . fingers . . . and again, epiphyseal union is noted, but that can take place from thirteen years onwards . . . Again no degenerative disease like arthritis is noted . . . and so from the eleven bones my assessment is that these bones are from a young adult, possibly in his or her twenties. Now we turn to the skull. This is definitely male, it is large . . . massive in fact, heavier eyebrow ridges, the chin is more square and the mandible is heavier than would be the case were it the skull of a female. I note that the suture lines are closed, not a foolproof method of ageing – many variations and exceptions – but complete fusion, as in this case, could point towards a person or persons who were at least in their mid thirties when they died.'

'So the bones and the skull have a separate origin?' Hennessey asked. 'I mean separate as in from different people?'

'It would seem so . . . definitely a male skull, possibly female bones . . . but we are looking at age at the moment, we'll come on to sexing. The mandible is loose . . . nothing particularly unusual in that, rigor is caused by stiffening of the muscles, and all tissue has been lost, but I would expect some fusion of the bone joints . . . it's noticeably loose.' Dr D'Acre picked up the skull with her left hand and opened and closed the jaw with her right. Hennessey saw the image as grotesque, as if the skull was talking, or laughing. 'You see, it's very fluid . . . there is no resistance to speak of. The indication, the impression is that someone has done this before me, and quite recently.'

'I see,' Hennessey said, for want of something to say, but found the thought of somebody opening and closing the jaw of a skull disquieting. The case was opening up . . . two to twelve persons represented in the bones, the way they were left, as if to be found . . . and now the playing games with the skull.

'Now we turn to the mouth . . . well, recent and British dental work is noticed. That should help you, Mr Hennessey . . . in his identification I mean. There will still be dental records if he was killed less than eleven years ago.'

'Eleven years?'

'Dental records have to be kept for eleven years by law . . . after that, it's up to the whim of the dentist. But, as I said, this appears recent, less than eleven years old I would say, but you will need to get an odontologist to look at these teeth and dental work for a qualified opinion. It seems to be fairly unremarkable dentistry, no costly work . . . doesn't mean anything at all of course, but costly work would have indicated this gentleman to have been monied. He could still of course have been monied but chose not to have dosh spent on his gob.'

Hennessey smiled. It was unusual for Dr D'Acre to lapse into colloquialisms. She was clearly in good humour.

'So, let's move to sexing the bones.' She took the femur and stood it upright on the table. It inclined at a distinct angle. 'This is about the only determination of sex I can make, with the only one of these bones that I can do it with.' She studied the bone. 'You see, if you stand the femur on its condoyles on a flat surface it inclines as you see. It's not possible to stand a femur upright. This is called the collodiaphyseal angle. The collodiaphyseal angle differs between the sexes and the difference is caused by the wider, childbearing pelvis of the female causing the female femur to slope more markedly than the male in order for them to meet at the knees . . . so, if the angle exceeds fifty degrees from the vertical, as this one clearly does, there is an eighty per cent chance of it being female. So at least one female is represented in these bones . . . and the skull is large . . . he would have been a big-faced man in life, not a small face, yet the two right sternal clavicles are on the small size . . . female . . . so at least two women, if the femur and one of the clavicles belonged to the same person. As I said, it will be DNA testing which will determine how many once living and breathing souls are represented by these bones. So . . . race . . . ethnic grouping . . . The bones will not tell us but the skull will tell us more . . . possibly. Racial mixing has caused some confusion and it's difficult to tell Asian and European skulls apart, but not impossible. Well, the teeth are not Mongoloid . . . they have upper and lower incisors and the width of the skull tends to thinness, not to width. So I think we can safely say he is not Oriental. The Afro-Caribbean race has eye orbits which are lower and wider than these orbits; the Afro-Caribbean nasal aperture is wider than the aperture here and the mandible is more modest than would be the case in an Afro-Caribbean gentleman. So . . . white . . . but whether Alpine, Nordic or Mediterranean . . . being the three subdivisions of the white race, I can't tell.' Dr D'Acre picked up the femur. 'This would be straighter than it is if it was the femur of an Afro-Caribbean female.'

'So at least one white adult male, one white adult female.' Hennessey summed up the findings to date. 'And ten, anything up to ten others?'

'Yes . . . quite a headache for you. So let's see what we can determine about height. The skull tells us nothing about the height of the man, but it is fair to surmise he was possibly tall . . . no, no, I can't say that . . . I have seen small, but powerfully built men with large faces . . . so I won't say that. The only bone that can help us is the femur, which has been most useful this morning. This is fraught . . . a skeleton is probably less than the living person by one inch, cartilage shrinking, decay of foot and scalp tissue . . . and after the age of thirty we shrink by about point six millimetres per year. It's a rule of thumb that a femur is twenty-seven per cent the length of the overall height. And I emphasize rule of thumb, Mr Hennessey.'

'Understood, Dr D'Acre.'

Dr D'Acre took a retractable tape measure and measured the femur. 'It's approximately sixteen inches long, or about forty-one centimetres . . . so that would make this lady about five feet six inches tall . . . in Imperial language, or a hundred and sixty-eight centimetres . . . and that is approximate, with a capital "A". You accept that?'

'I do.'

'Well, I'll only be tied to what I say in my report, Mr Hennessey, and in my report I will emphasize that those are approximations. Could be a few inches out . . . but she was of average height . . . not overly tall, not unduly short.'

'It all helps . . . and I am grateful.'

'Well, quite a bag of bones. No injuries are in evidence . . . the femur might contain traces of poison. I'll test for that of course, but it's rare to find it. Loved by the

Victorians but not so easily obtained and easily traceable. And how old are the remains? Well, the dentistry is recent and the body can be reduced to a skeletal state in a matter of weeks in the UK . . . a matter of days in the tropics, if outdoors and not contained in anything that keeps insects and scavengers away. So you have three, or twelve persons here . . . at least one man and one woman definitely . . . the second clavicle is almost certainly also female . . . so one man, two women . . . the metacarpals could be of either sex.' She paused. 'I'll send them all back to Wetherby for DNA testing.'

'Thanks. There were no prints on them or the bag . . . the only prints came from the person who found them. He's known to us and was last seen trying to be inter-viewed by the TV crew . . . but only for money . . . and he was not having much luck. The appeal for information went out yesterday.'

'Yes, I saw it.'

'No response yet and the door-to-door inquiry produced nothing, but that's Cambridge House. They don't like the police, those folk who live there.'

'Well, I'll get scrubbed off . . . grab some lunch . . . I'll write my report this p.m. I'll fax it to you as soon as it's been typed up. You might even receive it before close of play today. Depends how busy my secretary is.'

'That would be very useful. Very useful indeed.'

'All part of the service. I imagine it will be legwork for you now, Inspector.'

'I imagine it will,' Hennessey nodded. 'I imagine it will.'

'Well, it's one of ours.' The woman looked at the bag, which was contained within a clear cellophane production sachet. 'Or rather, was.'

'Was?' Yellich shifted his position on the chair.

'Yes, was . . . it's an outdated design. We felt it looked

dark . . . we don't want to be too bright . . . we are an upmarket shop.'

'That's what my boss said about the bag. That's the very observation he made yesterday.'

'Really? We are transmitting the correct message then. Good.'

The woman, Sandra Harcourt, by the nameplate on her brushed aluminium, very twenty-first century desk, seemed pleased. 'It was my idea to use darker colours rather than light colours. I can tell the board it worked.' She wore a powerfully loud red dress which Yellich thought contrasted somewhat with her attitude towards light colours. Her hair was short but neatly and expensively cut, her face was, to Yellich's taste, plastered with make-up, and her finger-nails were equally loudly red, matching her dress perfectly. Sandra Harcourt's office was similarly 'loud' in colour, further contrasting with her choice of colour for the company's shopping bags. A red carpet, a softer red than her dress or nail varnish, but red nonetheless, covered the floor, the wallpaper was purple velveteen with twirls of gold and prints of men and women on horses dressed in hunting pink hung in dark-stained wooden frames. The window looked out towards the railway station on the far side of the River Ouse. The office smelled heavy with artificial fragrance and Sandra Harcourt's cologne.

'You don't use the bag any more?'

'The design, you mean? No, we don't. As I said, we now have a lighter coloured design. This design is about two years old.'

'Two years?'

'Yes. I confess I quite fell out of my chair when I saw it on the regional news last evening . . . and so this is the very bag the bones were found in?' She turned the bag over in her hands as if driven by morbid curiosity.

'The very one.' Yellich paused. 'I really don't know

what you can tell us, if anything. It's a bit of a long shot. If it was a bag from a high street chain with multiple outlets, we probably wouldn't have followed it up . . . but nobody knew Whitelands, we looked you up in the *Yellow Pages*.'

'And you . . . you are an Inspector?'

'Sergeant,' Yellich said. 'I am a Detective Sergeant.'

'Ah . . . well, I am not displeased by that. Whitelands is a clothiers for discerning ladies only . . . Our customers do not step off the street and buy something, they travel many miles for the specific purpose of making a purchase.'

'I see.'

'And this bag certainly came from us . . . this shop . . . there is only one Whitelands in the United Kingdom, but our bags are solid as you see, they have a long shelf life . . . they are very popular among small shopkeepers.'

'I don't follow?'

'Well, once madam has conveyed her purchase home, she has no further use of the bag, and we understand that madam's husband often offers the bag to newsagents or to the owners of beer offs to enable their customers to carry their purchases home. I understand the term is "recycling". So while this bag definitely came from this very building, the person who used it to carry the bones in may well have obtained it from a newsagent to carry his papers home in on a wet Sunday morning, or to carry his wine home in from the beer off. I come from Sheffield.' Sandra Harcourt smiled. 'Uniquely in the United Kingdom, in Sheffield "beer offs" are what everyone else calls "off sales".'

'Ah . . . I was going to ask what a "beer off" was.'

'Well, now you know. A localized different name for a very common animal.'

'So we can't make that strong a link with the bag and this shop?'

'I am afraid not, Sergeant, especially since it's at least two years old, and possibly five years old . . . quite a long life for a plastic bag. What I can tell you though is that this is the largest bag we use . . . scarves, lingerie, would be placed in smaller bags, as would hats and nylons and shoes . . . we do a small range of shoes. Blouses and skirts we would place in the intermediate size bag, but this bag was used to carry home a dress or a coat.'

'It's too much to hope that you keep records of your sales?'

Sandra Harcourt shook her head. 'No . . . it's not too much to hope at all. Whitelands likes to know who its customers are. We make receipts out to the customer's name and address. And we keep the records for fifteen years. It's just that sort of establishment.'

Yellich sat back in his chair, smiling a broad smile.

'But . . .' Sandra Harcourt held up a finger as if in warning, 'and it's a big "but" . . . we can't link this bag to any specific purchase.'

'Of course.'

'And while we can provide the receipts, they are kept in the attic . . . right above me. Can't keep anything in the cellar . . . this is York, and every year the gentle Ouse floods . . . sometimes vastly so, as you know. We can't get flood-damage insurance on this building . . . Theft and fire yes, but flood damage . . . We carry the cost of the damage ourselves, as do many homes and businesses which stand on the Ouse's flood plain. Anyway, the "but" is that you will have to provide the manpower. And there are hundreds of receipts to sift through. I can let you have the exact date we started using this design of bag and the exact date we stopped, which will give you a time window, but that's all I can do. Even then, you may not find the purchase concerned, because our customers very occasionally ask for a small item to be placed in a large bag:

they want a large bag for some personal recycling purpose, or they want to walk to their car carrying a large Whitelands bag to give the impression that they have made an expensive purchase, when all the bag contains is a box of handkerchiefs. Whether you think that that is worth the manpower is really up to you.'

'Thankfully, it's really up to my boss. But he's a very thorough man, he may think it worth it.'

'Well, it's large but not unmanageable. You may have noticed that there were no customers in the shop when you arrived . . . It's like that sometimes, not a customer, not a sale for days at a time . . . and we often sell to a few customers whom we know well, time and time again, so a number of those receipts will pertain to the same household. We sell perhaps one or two coats or dresses each week on average . . . really, we are kept financially buoyant by our lingerie range . . . small bags, except occasionally when a larger bag is requested for whatever reason, as I said. So two per week for three years . . . about three hundred receipts, but those three hundred receipts might represent about thirty or forty households.'

'A faint but distinct light at the end of the tunnel.'

'Or a light beyond these woods as my American friends would say.'

The clock on her wall struck twelve.

The phone on Hennessey's desk rang its soft warbling tone. He let it ring twice, then picked it up.

'DCI Hennessey.'

'Switchboard, sir.'

'Yes?'

'Caller on the line . . . wants to talk to the officer in charge of the "Bag of Bones" case.'

'Oh . . . put him through, please.' Hennessey waited.

'Hello . . .' The voice sounded timid, it was faint.

'Yes, DCI Hennessey speaking. I understand you want to talk about the "Bag of Bones" case?'

'This is Horace . . .'

'Yes, Horace.' Hennessey leaned forward.

'He did it . . . couldn't stop him.'

Then the line went dead. Hennessey replaced the phone. It was, he believed, a crank call: happens all the time.

Two

in which Hennessey visits an elderly lady and Yellich follows a trail.

George Hennessey scanned the list of names. All males, all white Europeans who had been reported missing in the York area in the last eleven years aged over 35. There were five names. Nearly one every two years on average; one person just disappearing, each leaving a family to grieve or to find ways of coping with the distress of not knowing what had happened to their brother, son, father, husband. Or perhaps they were just isolated, completely and wholly alone in the world. Five names, and those five names were only those reported missing to the police in York, where they had lived. The skull could have been that of an outsider.

Hennessey placed the list on his desk and picked up Dr D'Acre's report about the post-mortem, which had been faxed for his attention and which he had found in his pigeonhole when he arrived at Micklegate Bar Police Station at 08.30 that morning. In the report, Dr D'Acre repeated the observation that she had made during the post-mortem, that the dentistry 'appeared recent' and further added that she thought it was 'less than eleven years old'. That, thought Hennessey, had narrowed the

24

field down quite nicely. He felt he was able to further narrow the field down by examining the photographs of the 'mis pers'. One man had a boxer's flattened nose and because he had smiled for his photograph, which was subsequently given to the police, Hennessey could tell at a glance that all his front teeth, both top and bottom incisors, had been lost. The man had had a criminal record for violence and Hennessey felt that his teeth had probably been lost on a pub floor or in the showers in prison. Further, he felt that if he was missing, given the people he associated with, then he would remain missing . . . his body would never be found. Nonetheless, whatever had happened to the man, his missing teeth enabled Hennessey to exclude him from the list of possible names.

Another man on the list, tragically just thirty-five years old, had a last known address which was that of a hostel for down-and-outs . . . not Hennessey pondered, likely to be a man who takes good care of his teeth. The most perplexing disappearance of those five 'mis pers' was the 45-year-old used-car salesman, one very 'Flash Harry', Hennessey felt . . . that small face, those white teeth, the gold pen in the jacket pocket, the gold decorations on his fingers, the gold bracelet. He, in Hennessey's opinion, would be just the sort of man to have gold-capped fillings. He placed that man's file on one side and mentally removed his name from the list.

That left him with just two names of people, both males, in the age range that Dr D'Acre had estimated the skull to belong, who had disappeared in the greater York area in the last eleven years. One was called Henry Fulwood, and the other was one Nigel Wright, 37 and 42 years of age respectively when they were reported missing. Neither man had acquired a police record; one was single, the other was a family man, and neither seemed particularly wealthy, both the sort of man who would have plain, simple fillings on the National Health Service, if possible. Both photographs of the two men were conveniently full faced, easily superimposed on a photograph of the skull. If one fitted, if the eye sockets, the jaw and the nasal aperture all matched, then it would be sufficient to deem that identification had been achieved. One family would be informed, one family could begin to grieve, the other, or both families, would have to continue to live with the anguish of not knowing what had happened to their missing son, in the case of Henry Fulwood, or their missing husband, in the case of Nigel Wright.

Hennessey detached the photographs from the files and sent them by police motorcycle courier to the Department of Pathology at York District Hospital with the request that they be matched against the skull found with eleven bones, on the eleventh-floor landing of Cambridge House. He had returned the other files to the void, knowing they could be extracted again if both the two photographs proved to be a negative match. If all ten photographs proved to be a negative match, then other lines of inquiry would have to be pursued. Hennessey glanced out of the small window of his office and saw a small group of tourists huddled under umbrellas as they walked the ancient walls of the city. He thought they looked perplexed, as if wondering what they were doing braving rain to walk on flagstones, going on holiday in the winter of the year.

His phone rang. He waited for it to ring twice, then slowly picked it up and in a calm voice he said, 'DCI Hennessey.'

'Dr D'Acre for you, sir.'

'Thank you.' Hennessey heard the line click and Dr Louise D'Acre's detached and emotionless voice said, 'Hello?'

'Yes. Hello . . .' Hennessey speaking.

'I've just completed the analysis of the tooth . . . taken from the skull.'

'Ah . . . I have just sent two photographs over to you for comparison, taken from our mis pers files . . . just to prosecute the investigation. I had a look at our mis pers and only two seemed likely.'

'I see. Was one about thirty-seven years old?'

'I believe one was, yes.'

'Well, that's the age at death of the person whose skull this is . . . thirty-seven, plus or minus twelve months.'

'That's very interesting. If you could ask your photographer to try to match the photograph of Henry Fulwood . . . he was thirty-seven when he disappeared . . . the other chap was in his forties.'

'No point in matching him then . . .'

'None . . . but Fulwood's the correct age. If it isn't him, we'll have to go nationwide . . . publicize it, contact the National Missing Persons Helpline.'

'Yes . . . it's astounding we have to rely on a charitable organization to catalogue missing persons on a nationwide basis, that's really something the police should organize . . . in my humble opinion.'

'In mine too,' Hennessey said, 'but in my waters, I think we've got a result here.'

'Well, I'll phone you in about an hour's time, let you know if your waters are correct.' She replaced the handset. Hennessey said 'thanks' into a dead phone, and replaced his own handset.

Ninety minutes later, Dr Louise D'Acre phoned back. The photograph of Henry Fulwood matched perfectly with the photograph taken of the skull. The skull itself, she reminded him, was still at the forensic laboratory at Wetherby for DNA testing. 'But it's a match,' she said. 'It's definitely a match.'

'Which will enable us to move on,' Hennessey said. 'Though bad news will have to be broken.'

'Well, if it helps, Chief Inspector, were I Henry Fulwood's next of kin, I would prefer to know, rather than be left wondering.'

'As I would. But thanks . . . You'll be confirming this in writing?'

'Of course . . . with the photographs attached for proof.'

Linda Handy remained silent. She looked at the man dressed in the blue shirt and jeans and soft shoes. Through the opaque glass window at her side she could see the comforting white blur of the prison officer's uniform, comforting because this man could be violent and he had nothing to lose. She had entered the room having surrendered anything that could be used as a weapon, pens, her bag . . . even her jewellery.

'They argue.' The man broke the silence.

'Who?'

He shrugged. He was small, slightly built. There was a noticeable absence of threat about his presence, so noticeable that Linda Handy had to remind herself that this man, who looked like a newspaper seller, had murdered ten people. It was his harmless-seeming presence that had enabled him to get close enough to do it, and it was his harmless-seeming presence that had enabled him to elude the suspicions of the police until he was arrested when in the process of claiming victim number eleven. 'Them . . .' He pointed to his head.

'Them?'

'Aye . . . them . . . Well, it's why I'm in here, isn't it?' He looked about him. 'Mind, it's a softer touch than prison, got more freedom . . . up to a point, but the walls are the same . . . the outside walls I mean. I'll never get out.'

'Tell me about "them"?'

'I was fifteen, I felt I was arguing with myself.'

'Yes.' Linda Handy nodded. 'It starts like that and about that age too . . .'

'Does it?'

'Yes.'

'It's like fighting all the time . . . in my head . . . no two like each other.'

'Well you see, that's what we have to do . . . we have to stop them fighting.'

'Is that possible?'

'Well . . . yes, frankly.'

'It's been done with other patients then?'

'Yes.' She smiled. 'You see, it used to be the case that psychologists and psychiatrists would attempt to blend the personalities into one, but that never worked . . . so now we try to get them to live with each other.'

'Which is what you are doing?'

'Which is what I will be trying to do.'

'Well, we've got plenty of time. I'm in here for life.'

'Well . . . we don't want to take that long, you're still a young man.'

'Twenty-three . . .'

'We don't want to take fifty years over it.'

'How will it work?'

'The method . . . talking, like this . . . just the two of us.'

'And the screw outside.'

'Yes, but he can't hear anything and the room isn't bugged . . . and later, you could be introduced to a group.'

'A group?'

'Other patients . . . really this session is just to meet each other . . . and we'll try and meet weekly for an hour.'

'Try?' The man became aggressive.

'Public holidays and other commitments will interrupt the timetable a little . . . but we'll plan for weekly.'

'OK.' The man relaxed. He paused. 'You know what makes me angry about this is the sense that I didn't do it.'

'Who did?'

'Ken . . . he's a murderous animal . . . he causes the trouble in here.' He tapped the side of his head. 'It's him that upsets the others . . . me and Barry and David . . . we get on OK . . . but Ken . . . he causes all the bother and it was Ken that did them old women . . . wouldn't listen to us . . . we couldn't stop him.'

'Well perhaps I'll meet Ken . . . one day.'

'He keeps himself well back.'

'Can I meet Ken now?'

The man's face screwed up, then he shook his head, 'No . . . no . . . you can't.'

'Perhaps next week?'

'Perhaps.' The man stood, he tapped on the door.

'We've got another thirty minutes.'

'Yes . . . I want back to the ward . . . but next week . . .'

'Very well, we'll see each other next week.'

Hennessey drove out of York along Haxby Road to Rowan Crescent, New Earswick. He parked his car at the entrance to the crescent, where it joined Rowan Avenue, and walked along the crescent. New Earswick was designed and built as a 'model' or 'garden' village, and to Hennessey's eye had all the appearance of a council estate. The roads were too narrow and allowed insufficient parking space, so much so that Hennessey realized that if a house caught fire, any fire appliance would be obliged to plough through the parked cars in order to reach the blaze. Hennessey turned up his coat collar against the wind. He glanced upwards: the cloud was at 9/10ths in RAF speak, but high. The rain, he thought, would hold off. He walked along Rowan

Crescent until he reached number 27, and turned into a narrow path which ran alongside what he had to concede was a very neatly tended garden, to the blue-painted front door, and knocked with the brass door knocker. There was no clear response from within, though Hennessey believed he may have heard a noise. He waited and knocked again. In response to his second knock, a woman's voice called out, 'Go round the side.' Hennessey walked from the front door further down the path as it ran alongside the house, to the other door. He stood in front of it but yet at a deferential distance from it. He didn't want to be an intimidating presence when the householder, who sounded elderly, opened the door. The door was eventually pulled open, partially so, by a frail-looking woman, who pushed her face between the door and the frame. She blinked at Hennessey. 'Yes?'

'Police.' Hennessey showed her his ID. 'Don't be alarmed.'

'Oh . . .' The elderly lady visibly relaxed and opened the door a little wider. 'There's been break-ins on the estate, old people get invaded and Mrs Hamilton had a heart attack when they broke into her house.'

'Yes . . . I have heard of that gang, we are looking for them.'

'You are not looking very hard . . . they do it in broad daylight.'

'Yes . . .' Hennessey nodded, 'so I have heard.' But the woman's response told him that whilst her body had wasted, her mind was still there, still as sharp as a tack. 'You are Mrs Fulwood?'

'I am.'

'Well, may I come in? I have some news for you.'

'About Henry?'

'Yes . . .'

'You've found him?'

31

'If I could come in?'

Mrs Fulwood's house seemed to Hennessey to be small but very homely, very cosy; it smelled of furniture polish and every item seemed to be where it should be. He doubted that, with her evident frailty, Mrs Fulwood would be able to keep such a neat and well-ordered home and, scanning the room, he read 'Home Help' provided by the Social Services two or three times per week. Mrs Fulwood walked stiffly towards a high-backed chair which stood at the side of a hissing gas fire. She turned and lowered herself into it, gasping with pain as she did so. 'Arthritis,' she said, 'it comes and goes. Well, no it doesn't, it's always with me . . . but some days it's worse than others.'

'I'm sorry.'

'What for? Hardly your fault . . . and it's a disease of old age, so I tell myself. You can live a long life and get arthritis, or you can die young and not get arthritis . . . Me, I'd prefer to live long enough to get arthritis.'

Hennessey smiled. He liked her attitude.

'So, you have found Henry? Do sit down.' Mrs Fulwood pointed to an armchair which stood on the opposite side of the gas fire.

Hennessey removed a copy of *People's Friend* from the cushion and placed it in a magazine rack which stood between the chair and the wall. He then sat as invited. 'Well . . . Mrs Fulwood, the news is not good . . .'

'He's dead?'

'Well, yes . . . I am afraid so.' Hennessey leaned forward. He avoided eye contact with Mrs Fulwood, looking down and to his left and the modest flame of the gas fire. The fire was set to minimum, clearly in order to save money, and managed only to take the edge off the chill of the room rather than heat it.

'I didn't expect him to return, not after this length of time. He was a good boy. There was only ever the two of us . . . we were quite close. He always let me know where he was going, what he was doing . . . he was that sort of boy. It was hard for him growing up without a father . . . a boy needs a father to look up to. His father was in the Territorial Army, he was killed on an exercise. About this time of year, four of them were going down the Ouse in a rubber dinghy . . . at night . . . the thing overturned, they were weighed down with heavy kit in icy water . . . one of them survived, managed to reach the bank . . . the other three . . . my husband and two others . . . were drowned.'

'I'm sorry.'

'Well, that's not your fault either, but thank you. Terence was such a lovely man. That's his photograph.' She pointed to a framed photograph which stood on her cluttered mantelpiece. 'He was warm and generous. I could never replace him, so I didn't try. Henry grew up to be like him as well. Without his father being there he grew up to be warm and generous. So tell me what you have come to tell me.'

'Very well. You can also help us get justice for Henry by answering questions.'

'Justice?' Mrs Fulwood gasped. 'He didn't die accidentally?'

'Well, it appears not, Mrs Fulwood.' Hennessey paused. 'You may have to brace yourself for some bad news.'

'Go on.'

She was indeed, Hennessey thought, a woman of grit. 'Well . . . not all of his body was found.'

'Oh . . .' Mrs Fulwood lurched forward and gripped the wooden arms of the chair in which she sat, with hands and fingers which were white and twisted. 'What did you find?'

'His skull.' There seemed to be no easier way of saying it, no gentler way, though Hennessey spoke as softly as he could.

'His skull?' Mrs Fulwood looked at Hennessey, holding eye contact with him, as if appealing for some sense to be made of the news, some explanation, some rationale.

'Just his skull.'

'Well, how do you know it's Henry? . . . It could be anybody's skull.'

'Skulls might look the same, but they are different . . . the small differences in dimension in the bone from skull to skull get accentuated when layers of muscle and skin are laid on them . . . A bit like a lump in a carpet – it looks as big as a golf ball, but when you lift the carpet you find the lump is caused by something much smaller. Whatever it is is pushing up the layers of carpet and making it appear larger than it is. But that's why we all have different faces . . . small differences in bone measurements, which are not noticeable if you place one skull against another. Anyway, the medical photographers at York District Hospital were able to place a photograph of the skull over the photograph of Henry that we have in the missing persons' file, and it matches . . . the eye sockets, the nose cavity . . . the jaw line. I am very sorry.'

'There is no mistake? I have come to accept Henry is dead, but I had hoped for a whole body to bury . . . to put with his father.'

'Well, we could confirm it with dental records, if you could let me know which dentist Henry saw.'

'Mr Wheatman, in Gillygate.'

Hennessey took out his notepad and wrote, 'Wheatman, dentist, Gillygate'. He kept the pad open. 'The missing person report gives little information about Henry, anything you can tell us would be helpful.'

'Well, he was my son, what can I tell you? He just didn't come home one night.'

'Was he employed?'

'He was in a sort of on-and-off way. He left school and went to sea . . . He could never settle after that, drifted from one job to another with periods on the dole . . . Never got into bother though, you know, Mr . . . ?'

'Hennessey.'

'Yes . . . Mr Hennessey, there is an awful lot of truth in the saying that the Devil makes work for idle hands. A lot of the unemployed men and women on this estate get into trouble with the police because they have nothing to occupy their time, but my Henry was never like that. Well, he wasn't, otherwise I'd have the police at my door but I never did. He'd sit reading . . . go out into York for the day to the library, come home . . . stay in if he hadn't any money. When he was working, he'd go out for a beer or two, with his mates, but he never got drunk. He'd come home, his breath would smell a bit but his behaviour was the same as when he was sober . . . dare say that's something else he inherited from his father . . . hollow legs. His father could drink all night long and it never seemed to affect him.'

'Was he working when he disappeared?'

'Aye, he was that . . . steadiest job he ever had since coming back from sea. He was a milkman . . . loved it . . . those early mornings, the streets to himself. I really thought he'd settled.'

'Which dairy?'

'Yorkshire Dairies. He worked at the depot on Kitchener Street, off Haxy Road, delivered on this estate and on the Huntingdon estate.' She paused. 'Aye . . . I really thought he'd settled.'

'Friends?'

'None that I met . . . He knew some men down the pub, the George and Dragon on Haxby Road. He didn't wander too far . . . but I've known that . . . men who've travelled seem content to keep themselves in the same small area ... Henry was like that. He travelled the world as a merchant seaman, been in rough weather too ... I used to get postcards from all over ... New York, Sydney, Panama, Cape Town ... still got them in a shoebox upstairs. So, after ten years of wandering like that, my Henry was happy to live and work in the same area, ten-minute bike ride to work at four a.m. each day ... He worked seven days a week ... picked up his milk and his float and delivered here in these streets and over in Huntingdon, take the float back, finish midday, except on Fridays, when he collected the money. He would sleep in the afternoon and then go down to the George and Dragon, which is halfway between here and the dairy, in the early evening, like from five p.m. to seven, but always back here by eight and in his bed to get a full eight hours before he had to be up again the next morning. Just didn't move from this small area unless it was to go into York. Then one day he didn't come back. He finished the round, took his float back to the depot, connected it up to the electricity supply so the batteries were charged overnight and got on his bike to cycle home, and that's the last he was seen ... Broad daylight ... in the summer in the middle of York and he vanishes.'

'Did he have a lady friend?'

'Do you know, I think he did. He never told me about her, but I sensed he had someone ... he seemed content. I occasionally got the whiff of scent from his clothes. He'd come home at eight but sometimes there was no smell of beer on his breath, as if he'd been with his lady, whoever she was.'

'I see.'

'His skull?' Again Mrs Fulwood looked at Hennessey in that appealing manner. 'But where's the rest of him? Where's the rest of my Henry?'

'We'd like to know that too.'

'Oh . . .' She extended a white, misshapen hand to an ancient-looking television set which stood on a sideboard by the dining table. 'I heard the news . . . yesterday, or the day before . . . a bag of bones found somewhere. That's not my Henry?'

'Yes . . . that is where his skull was found.'

She paused. 'But if only his skull was found . . . who do all the other bones belong to?'

'We'd like to know that as well,' said Hennessey.

It was a smaller list than even Yellich could have hoped for. Thirty names, over a five-year period, had been given bags of the size that the bones had been found in, but as Mrs Sandra Harcourt explained, that's Whitelands – their clientele is small but very select. The thirty names accounted for the sale of 150 very expensive coats and/or dresses in the period in question. Some so ridiculously expensive, in Yellich's view, that one or two items were more costly than his annual mortgage repayments. He was aware, as Sandra Harcourt had pointed out, that the bag in which the bones had been found may not have been given to any of the names he had derived from Whitelands sales receipts. A woman might have purchased a scarf, a box of handkerchiefs, or similar, and asked to be given the largest of Whitelands' bags so that she might parade through the 'famous and fayre', giving the impression that she had purchased a coat or a dress worth hundreds, perhaps thousands of pounds, doubtless filling out the bag with a few items of shopping so as to carry off the illusion. That was a possibility he could not ignore, but neither could he ignore the possibility that one of the thirty names had been given the bag to be used by some other and that second person had given it to the person who had eventually used it to convey the twelve bones to the uppermost landing of Cambridge House. Having thanked Sandra Harcourt for her co-operation, Yellich had walked back through the medieval streets, taking a short cut through a snickelway, to Micklegate Bar Police Station. It was by then midday. He signed in, checked his pigeonhole and walked to his office in the CID corridor. As he passed Hennessey's office, he saw Hennessey at his desk and further noted that the Detective Chief Inspector, whose face was normally lined with age, looked more troubled than usual. He tapped on the doorframe. 'Boss?'

Hennessey glanced up and smiled as he ran the fingers of his liver-spotted hands through his silvery grey hair. 'Ah, Yellich. How did you get on at Whitelands?'

Yellich told him.

'So, some door-to-dooring for you?'

'"Door-to-dooring" is hardly the expression, skipper . . . more like long-drive-to-long-driving, going by these addresses . . . some prestigious-sounding piles here.' He glanced at the list. 'Cookham Hall . . . Bewley Manor . . . some houses just have names, then the village they're in . . . "Pekesands", Ashton in the Forest, Yorkshire, would you believe?'

Hennessey smiled. 'Far cry from Twenty-seven, Rowan Crescent, New Earswick, where I have spent much of the morning breaking bad tidings and getting a little bit of information.'

'Thought you looked a little crestfallen, skipper.'

'I feel it . . . but not because of that home visit to one Mrs Fulwood . . . elderly lady, but a brain that's all there . . . It's this.' He tapped the piece of paper he was holding. 'You'd better come and take a pew.' He indicated the chair which stood in front of his desk. 'Got the results from Wetherby,' he said as Yellich sat in the chair, 'it makes not good reading.'

'The DNA results on the bones?'

'The very same, the techno jargon is beyond me, it talks of ordinary DNA and mitochondrial DNA being extracted . . . the latter I believe can be used to trace the maternal line . . . The DNA, both types, was extracted from the marrow and the "Haversion system" of the bones. And frankly, the only thing I understand there is the word "marrow", because my dog chews the bones I give him to get to the marrow . . . but for us, the alarming news, and this is why I asked you to sit, because I was pleased I was seated when I read it, is that all twelve bones come from twelve different persons.'

'Oh . . .' Yellich groaned. 'Oh no, oh no.'

'Oh yes, oh yes, oh yes.' Hennessey placed the report on his desk. 'We have no reports over the years of graves being plundered, so we have to assume these are the bones of murder victims. It's a serial killer leaving us a present, and the worst type of serial killer . . . one that very quickly gets on with his job . . . and doesn't seek attention by leaving the bodies where they can be found. We have a skull, a female femur . . .'

'That's the leg bone?'

'Yes . . . two female clavicles . . . they're apparently the collarbone . . . and nine fingers, or what Dr D'Acre calls metacarpals.'

'Fingers will do for me, skipper.'

'Me as well . . . keep the speak simple speak.' Hennessey drew a deep breath. 'There is apparently no way of sexing fingers. So . . . one male, identified as Henry Fulwood . . . we'll have to get into that inquiry, it's a murder now; three females and a further nine that may be male or female . . . and all died at least two years ago because Wetherby informs us in this report that that is the least time that bone becomes completely skeletonized in our climate. Could be as long as ten years, depending on the amount of damp.'

39

'Going public with it, boss?'

'Yes, have to, I think, distressing as it will be to their relatives. So we know the identity of one. Who are the other eleven . . . and who's number thirteen?'

'Number thirteen, skipper?' Yellich raised a quizzical eyebrow.

'Number thirteen, Yellich, is the person or persons unknown who left us the present. He or she or they want to be caught.'

'Want to be caught?'

'Yes. The belief is that serial killers want to be caught, that they play the most terrible game of "catch" . . . but it's a game nonetheless. Saw photographs of a crime scene in the USA: a serial killer targeted women living alone, inveigled his way into their homes, murdered them, bloodily so, ransacked the house, then took their lipstick and wrote "Stop me before I do this again" on a dressing-table mirror.'

'Blimey!'

'As if the good and the bad of his personality were in constant conflict. Personally speaking, I think the Yorkshire Ripper wanted to be caught. He was stopped and questioned any number of times in Bradford, but he lived there . . . but by going to Sheffield where he had no business to be, he drew very close attention to himself. I think that was his way of giving himself up. Once in custody, he coughed quickly enough. I'll never know whether I am right or not but this, this act of leaving a bag of bones where they will be found is the action of someone who wants to be caught. In the meantime, he or she or they may or may not carry on killing.'

'I hadn't thought of that. What's for action?'

'Lunch. Meet me here at . . . one thirty. You'll be lunching in the canteen?'

'Have to, boss . . . it's cheap.'

'And nasty. One thirty, here.'

'One thirty. Very good, skipper.'

So they had discovered the bones. Good. The man thought that was good. It was all going to plan. He sat back in the chair and relaxed. He felt in control. It was good to be in control. He glanced out of the window at the flat landscape, the denuded trees, the scudding clouds. He would be out of here soon. Very soon. Now they will know that he means business . . . By now they will have found out that the twelve bones had come from twelve victims. He knew that DNA could be extracted from bones . . . they had even been able to extract DNA from the bones of the Romanov family, eighty years after they had been murdered, and even after their bones had been doused in petrol and set alight. Now he needed victim number thirteen.

WEDNESDAY, 13.37 HOURS – 17.35 HOURS

'Still don't know how you can eat that stuff. Cheap or not.' Hennessey sat back in his chair, and patted his stomach. 'Good pub grub . . . can't beat it. And it gets you out of the station.'

'Well, perhaps when I reach your rank, skipper, and if—'

'And my age.' Hennessey smiled. 'Now to business. I'll have to appraise the Commander of this.' He patted the file which had been opened in respect of the discovery of the bag of bones, and which had now been cross-referenced to the missing persons case of one Henry Fulwood. 'He's been away for the morning, attending a conference in Scarborough, as you probably know. So . . . your inquiries at Whitelands . . . do you think that will be profitable? Seems a bit of a red herring to me.'

41

'Well, boss . . .' Yellich sat forwards, holding his mug of tea in his hands. 'I'll take advice on it of course, but my thinking is that the bags are so rare, we won't find the murderer among the thirty households, that's for certain, they probably know the bags could be traced to them. But what I am hoping for, is for one or two households to tell me they always hand used plastic bags to a retailer . . . a small newsagent, an off sales, a charity shop . . . and the staff there might remember using the bag to put some person's purchase in. They wouldn't remember a Marks & Spencer bag, for example.'

'Because they are so common?'

'That's it . . . but a Whitelands bag . . . that might even be worthy of comment.'

'Yes.' Hennessey nodded and reached for his own mug of tea. 'I begin to see your logic. You are assuming that the great majority of the bags taken home by those thirty households will have been discarded in the domestic refuse but one or two householders, as you say, have clearly offered the bag for further use. Yes . . . alright, go with it, see where you get to but I may pull you off it if I think we should pursue a different line.'

'Very good, boss. Thanks.'

'Now I want to follow up on Henry Fulwood's disappearance. His elderly mother told me of his place of employment and a lady friend. Five years on now, but if we find his murderer, we find the murderer of the other eleven.' Hennessey paused. 'I'll prepare a press release. This will make the national newspapers, which is in our interest. In a case like this, we need all the publicity we can get.'

As Yellich expected, calling on the names gleaned from Whitelands' records was, in effect, calling on the stately homes of England. There were thirty addresses to be called at, widely dispersed across the Vale of York, but by plotting the location of each on a map and by calculating the most efficient route, he felt he could manage to call on three, perhaps four, each day. He felt that he would be able to visit all thirty addresses within ten working days. Not an unpleasant ten working days in the life of any police officer – all that personal space, just himself in the car, and even if the people on whom he would be calling were a bit 'nose in the air', they would at least be polite, well mannered and not at all antisocial or anti-police. All in all he anticipated a pleasant ten days' work. What he was totally unprepared for was that he got 'a result' on his first call.

He drove up the long gravel drive of Tewkesbury Hall, pondering the name, for the building was certainly large enough to merit the title of 'Hall' but it was, he thought, a long way from Tewkesbury in Gloucestershire. The family name being Thornton did not shed any light on the name of the building. He halted his car in front of the house, just to one side of the stone stairs which led up to the front door. The door of the house opened before he opened the door of his car.

'What do you want?' The owner of the voice was a small man, cold blue eyes and aggressive manner. He stood in the doorframe, dwarfed, it seemed to Yellich, by the doors. Yellich paused, then opened the car door slowly, in his own time, not being intimidated by the man. 'Police,' he said.

'Police!' The man turned and spat. Yellich had difficulty controlling his mirth. He was not amused by the man, but at himself. So much for spending ten working days calling on the toffee-noses who were at least well mannered, polite and not at all antisocial or anti-police.

'What do you want?' Yellich put the man's age as being mid thirties.

'A couple of questions.' Yellich walked towards the man.

'You've got nothing on me. Not any more. I've been inside for what I've done.'

'Really?'

'Yes, really, and this –' he pointed to the house – 'this is bought and paid for by honest sweat and no thanks to the likes of you.'

'I see.' Yellich began to walk up the steps.

'So what do you want now? I have an accountant now. All my books are in order now.'

'I'm sure they are. Your wife . . .'

'What about her?'

'She shops at Whitelands?'

'She shops wherever she wants to shop. She's a rich man's wife.'

'Lucky she.' Yellich smiled, but Thornton's icy blue eyes seemed to drill into him. He seemed to Yellich to be burning up with bitterness and having difficulty controlling pent-up rage. 'But she bought an item of clothing from Whitelands . . .'

'So?'

'We want to—'

'We? I only see one of you.'

'The police . . . want to trace the plastic bag she was given to carry her purchase home in.'

'Is that all you want?' Thornton smiled, as if relieved. 'I thought . . .'

'Yes . . . ?'

'Never mind.'

'What did you think?'

'I said never mind.' The smile was a brief interlude. The rage and bitterness resurfaced. But Thornton's fear of the police was real. He was up to something. Yellich would enter his name in the computer when he returned to Micklegate Bar, see what came up on the screen.

'So, do you know what you did with the bag?'

'If it went anywhere, it would have gone to my brother. He keeps a beer off in York. He likes beer . . . he's an expert and has a small beer off . . . an off sales in York, the "World Beer Centre", sells beers from all round the world. He's always in need of plastic bags, so we give him ours.'

'What's the address?'

'Look it up in the *Yellow Pages*.' Thornton turned and shut the door in Yellich's face. Yellich heard the sound of the slamming door echo inside the building.

Yellich called on two other houses in the vicinity of Tewkesbury Hall, where he was, as he'd expected, received with courtesy and with great apologies for being unable to be of assistance. Both householders, he was told, pursued the policy of consigning all plastic bags to the refuse. He returned to Micklegate Bar Police Station and there, as advised, he consulted the *Yellow Pages*. The 'World Beer Centre', listed under 'Off-licences', was in Holgate. He glanced out of his office window. The weather was holding. He would walk there.

He left the police station, angular and red brick, a distinct part of York's Victorian heritage which stood opposite the medieval, crossed Micklegate Bar, and walked into Blossom Street. He turned right into Holgate Road and, once over the railway bridge, he was in Holgate proper. This, he pondered, this was the part of the ancient city which the tourists never see, rows of black terraced houses with drying washing strung across the street, motorcycles chained to lampposts. He followed Holgate Road until it became Poppleton Road, then turned left into St Swithin's Walk. The World Beer Centre was in what Yellich saw to have been originally a corner shop. It still blended well, he thought, it looked like a corner shop still: a narrow door on the corner itself, large sheets of glass at ninety degrees to each other, one either side of the door, and the legend 'World Beer Centre' in modest, pastel shades, not large, loud and invasive. He pushed open the door, causing a single bell to chime. There was a counter; behind the counter were racks of spirits and tobacco, on the counter itself were trays of liquorice and opposite the counter stood a tall fridge with a see-through Perspex door which contained bottles of wine labelled according to price. Beyond the counter, deeper into the shop, were solid-looking wooden shelves containing bottled beer from many nations, from Africa, Singapore, but mainly so far as Yellich could see, they were beers from small English breweries with names like 'Old Peculier', 'Old Speckled Hen', 'Black Sheep', 'Pig's Nose'. A man emerged from the gloom of the stockroom beyond the racks of bottled beers. 'You'll be the police,' he said.

'Yes.' Yellich displayed no emotion.

'My older brother phoned me. He said you'd be calling on me.' The man's attitude seemed to Yellich to be the antithesis of his brother at Tewkesbury Hall. He was warm and welcoming; his brother had been cold and hostile. This man had a smooth face with straggly hair. The occupant of Tewkesbury Hall had a hard face, lined with worry and neatly cut hair. 'Something about a bag?'

'Yes . . . it's a long shot.' Yellich allowed himself to relax as he warmed to Thornton the younger. 'In fact it's about the longest long shot I have played.'

'If I can help you?' The man stood behind the counter and was able to hold eye contact with ease.

'Well . . . you'll have read about the bones . . . the bag of bones found at Cambridge House?'

'I watched the TV news, so yes, I know of them.'

'You saw the photograph of the bag they were found in?'

'Yes . . . a Whitelands bag.'

'Yes. That design was only used for a short period of time and the size was in the main only used for large purchases . . . I mean coats or dresses, not a large number of items.'

'Yes?'

'And in fact we were able to trace the likely purchasers of those purchases to thirty addresses in the Vale.'

'Is that all?'

'Some of the customers made more than one purchase, so there were more than thirty transactions.'

'I see, and one being my brother . . . or his wife?'

'Yes.'

'Well, they have the money to shop at Whitelands . . . he encourages her. She's a rich man's wife and he likes her to look the part and she doesn't complain.'

'I bet she doesn't.'

'So you've traced the bag to me?'

'Yes . . . hoping you might possibly remember who you gave it to.'

'I am sorry . . . a plastic bag.' Thornton knelt down and picked up a large plastic bag which was bulging with screwed-up plastic bags. He held it up. 'I need all the placcy bags I can get, my customers bring them in for me and my brother, my eldest brother, gives me the ones he's been given. I know my regular customers. I know what they are likely to buy, but I don't remember which bag I gave to which customer.'

'I appreciate that. If the bones had been found in a bag issued by a high-street store, we wouldn't have followed this line of inquiry, but a Whitelands bag, that's like a Harrods bag . . . we thought it might have provoked comment, or the fact that it was quite large, so large that a bottle of wine by itself would look silly in it, that also might have provoked comment, but clearly it didn't.'

'Not any comment I can remember.'

'Do you work this shop alone?'

'Yes. Me and me . . . and, oh yes . . . there's me.' Thornton smiled and shrugged. 'I open about this time, late afternoon, and close at ten . . . obtain the stuff from the wholesalers in the early afternoon. It's not a bad life. My customers are a good mix of locals and students. I don't sell cheap wine so I don't get the alcoholics coming in. It's specialized "beer off" . . . or "off sales" . . . I am a Sheffield lad. In the steel city "beer offs" are what the rest of the UK call "off sales". I sell interesting beers so I get beer connoisseurs as well as folk wanting the odd bottle of wine, or cans to drink at home.' He paused. 'Not a bad life. I can sleep late in the mornings, I work for myself . . . but sometimes, I think I have wasted my opportunities, ending up as a shopkeeper.' He patted the bag full of screwed-up plastic bags. 'Especially when I think what my brothers have done. You've met Stanley and seen his house, Tewkesbury Hall, and my middle brother is in the Army, a regimental sergeant major, a career soldier. He loves the life. He's been all over the world, he's well paid and is going to collect an inflation-proof pension some day. Then there's me, a corner shopkeeper. But nobody tells me what to do and I sleep late, and I sleep, which is more than Stanley does . . . those business deals which might not go through . . . his house . . . Well, if it takes worry and stress to be able to afford a house like that, well maybe my little place in the country isn't so bad.'

'You live in the country?' Yellich smiled. 'Not above the shop?'

'No . . . there's a flat up there but I rent it to students, the entrance is round the side.' He pointed to his left. 'I live in a small bungalow which used to be a smallholding, just ten acres, producing market-garden produce . . . still heavily mortgaged but I am turning the ten acres into a garden. But I am still just a shopkeeper.'

'You've done better than many.'

'Thanks, that makes me feel better. Have you thought that any of the customers of Whitelands might be the culprit?'

'Too obvious.' Yellich pursed his lips. 'They'll know that Whitelands has their addresses and the bag could be traced to them. We think our best hope is to go one step further and try to follow the recycling trail. Well, thanks anyway.'

Yellich returned to Micklegate Bar Police Station. At his desk he picked up his phone and pressed a four-figure internal number.

'Collator.' The response was crisp, instant.

'DS Yellich.'

'Yes, sir?'

'Stanley Thornton, Tewkesbury Hall, Howden in the Vale . . .'

'Yes, sir?'

'I called on him today, he doesn't like the police very much, can you tell me why?'

'Will you hold, sir?'

'Yes.' Yellich held and listened to the sound of a computer keyboard being tapped.

'Yes, he's known alright, sir . . . serious assault, embezzlement, served time in Full Sutton and Durham.'

'Durham!'

'Yes, sir . . . not a pleasant character. Durham's very, very selective about who they take.'

'Oh . . . I know.' Yellich allowed his smile to be heard down the phone.

'Active to DS Braithwaite of South Yorkshire CID.'

'Active?'

'That's what it says, sir.'

'Interesting. Do you have a phone number for DS Braithwaite?'

The collator read out a contact number and Yellich scribbled it on his pad. On a whim he asked if anything was known about Thornton's younger brother . . . he couldn't give a Christian name or address.

'He has siblings . . . says here, both younger. Horace, he's the youngest . . .'

'Saw him just now . . . owns an off sales.'

'He's got a little bit of track, receiving stolen goods . . . nothing in the last five years. The middle brother . . . Norman . . . no record at all. He's kept his nose clean.'

'Yes, he went for a soldier. Sounds like he saved himself from a police record by doing so. Thanks.' Yellich replaced the phone and picked it up again. He dialled nine for an outside line and then the number of DS Braithwaite in South Yorkshire.

'Just a courtesy call really,' Yellich said after he had been connected to Braithwaite and had identified himself. 'Had occasion to call on one Stanley Thornton of Tewkesbury Hall today.'

'Oh aye?' Braithwaite had a thick Yorkshire accent.

'Yes. He was hostile, found out why when I came back. Thought I'd better tell you I visited.'

'Aye.'

'He's not a suspect with us.'

'Aye . . . well, he is with us. He's up to his armpits in something mucky going on in this city.'

'Really? He seemed relieved when he found out he wasn't under suspicion.'

'Aye . . . well, he's under suspicion alright. Reckons he made his pile in scrap metal . . . he's got a small scrap yard as a front but there's graft and corruption going on here and he's involved, just can't pin him to anything.'

'I see.'

'Well, he's active in our turf, but lives in yours. If the investigation moved to your turf we'd notify you, but he seems to keep his criminal activities confined to Sheffield, which is his home town.'

'I see . . . I see. Well, if we can be of any assistance?'

'Aye . . .' And with that, DS Braithwaite put his phone down.

'Aye,' Yellich said into an empty phone, then he too replaced the handset. 'Aye.'

It was Wednesday, 17.35 hours.

Three

*in which Yellich makes a difficult house call,
Hennessey visits a dairy, a pub, and a church . . .
and victim number thirteen is taken.*

George Hennessey stood by the electric kettle which
stood on a table in the corner of his office. As he
waited for the kettle to boil he looked out of the window,
at the walls at Micklegate Bar, at tourists ambling along
the walls, at a local man, clearly a local, hurrying along
the walls, knowing, as only local people know, that walking
the walls is the speediest way to traverse the city.
Hennessey felt uplifted by the weather: it was still cold
outside, but the clouds had lifted in the night and that
Thursday had dawned clear and still. A still photograph
of the scene would, he thought, suggest a summer's day,
the impression would only be betrayed by the well
wrapped-up folk on the wall. The kettle boiled, he poured
the boiling water over the mix of instant coffee granules
and milk in the bottom of his mug and carried the drink
back to his desk. As he waited for the coffee to cool, he
thought of the previous afternoon.

It had been as he had expected it to be: like playing
an old and very familiar piece of music, or listening to
a favourite poem being recited. Note for note, word for

word, even pause for pause, he knew what was coming next. He'd walked into Commander Sharkey's office and had accepted the invitation to take a seat. The Commander, as always, was meticulously dressed, a short man for a police officer, with a neatly kept desktop and behind him, mounted on the wall, were two photographs, one he always said that he was proud of, of himself in the uniform of a junior officer in the British Army, and one he always said that he was less proud of – 'keeping it is like serving a penance' – of himself in the uniform of an officer in the Royal Hong Kong Police, as it once was. He had appraised the Commander of the 'Bag of Bones' inquiry and agreed with him that Yellich's idea to trace the onward life of the Whitelands bags to be a little unrealistic but had allowed it because of Yellich's enthusiasm for the idea. He added that he intended to redirect Yellich's efforts the following day, having already decided that Yellich's idea was a poor use of valuable police time.

The Commander had thanked Hennessey for a succinct appraisal and had asked to be kept informed of any developments. It was then that the old familiar piece of music or piece of poetry had been played/recited: the sorrowful story of Johnny Taighe, the maths teacher at the Commander's school, who smoked like a chimney and had a big red nose, indicating a drink problem, was dangerously overweight and in his last year of employment, when he should have been allowed to coast but instead the pressure was piled on, had keeled over one evening at home with a massive coronary. Dead, it was said, before he hit the ground. 'That won't happen in this nick while I sit at this desk, George,' and Hennessey, as always, when Sharkey chanted the mantra about the luckless Johnny Taighe, had held up his hand, stopping the Commander in mid sentence, though politely so, and had said, 'Thank you, but I am not under pressure. Close to retirement, yes, but well on top of things. I don't want to police a desk, and yes, I would inform you if things got too much for me.'

Then there had come the second movement, the second stanza, the tale of how the Commander had allowed himself to become part of the corruption that was the dominant culture in the R.H.K.P – a dangerous admission for him to make, but made in the manner of a confession and made with much regret and remorse. Not corruption in the sense it is meant in the UK, of planting evidence for example, nothing active, but a passive form of corruption. A sergeant would tell him not to patrol a specific quarter of the colony on a particular night. He would do as requested and the following morning an envelope full of money, equivalent to one month's pay, would be in his desk drawer. He wasn't there very long, just a few months, he explained, and had pointed out that if he had refused to play the game, to go along with it . . . to go with the flow, he would be found floating with the blue dolphins with his throat slit. 'Couldn't cope with that happening here, George.' To which Hennessey had assured the Commander of his certainty that there were no 'bad apples' in 'the nick', he was certain of it, and, having reassured the worrying Commander that he was not 'burned out' and that there was no corruption at Micklegate Bar, he extended his courtesies and took his leave.

He had driven home, a little earlier than usual, under a sky which was beginning to cloud over, and was grateful to have escaped York before the rush hour. He had arrived at Easingwold at about 5 p.m., was met by an excited Oscar, who ran in circles of delight at his master's return home. Hennessey had made himself a deep pot of tea, poured a mug of it, added milk and walked out of the back door of his detached house and talked to the garden, telling it of his day, of the investigation just begun and, that done, had returned indoors. He'd supped on a simple but wholesome casserole and settled down in front of a gas fire and read a recently published account of the Battle of Normandy. He found the prose stifling, leaden in parts, and some of the claims contradicted other reading he had done on the battle; the complete absence of maps was, he felt, inexcusable. A book about a specific battle which contains no maps, he thought, was as a motorcar without wheels. The reviews he had felt were fair, 'for collectors only' had been one reviewer's curt dismissal of the piece, but he was a collector of military history, and the book had been purchased for his collection.

Later he'd fed Oscar and man and dog took their customary evening walk to the fields at the edge of the village and back, and later still, Hennessey had taken his own customary evening stroll into Easingwold for a pint of brown and mild at the Dove Inn, just one, before last orders were called. He had slept well and awoke nourished and was delighted to see the clouds had lifted, that the sky was again a clear blue with hardly a cloud to be seen. By 9 a.m., or a little later than was usual, he was sitting at his desk, cradling a cooling mug of coffee and pondering what was 'for action' that day. He drained the mug and stood to return it to the table in the corner as Yellich tapped on his doorframe.

'Morning, Yellich,' Hennessey smiled. 'You look not only refreshed after a good night's rest but mightly pleased with yourself.'

'Got a kind of result on the bag, skipper.'

'Really? Glad you mentioned that because I want to talk to you about it.'

'Oh?'

'Yes, take a pew.' Hennessey walked across his office, placed the mug by the kettle and returned to his desk as Yellich accepted the invitation to sit down, looking, thought Hennessey, a trifle worried. 'Don't look so crestfallen.'

'Sorry, skipper,' Yellich smiled, 'must be my guilty conscience.'

'Well . . . it's nothing to worry about, but both the Commander and myself feel that trying to trace the bag's last owner is a fanciful line of inquiry. But you say you got a result?'

'Oh . . . well, a kind of result. I visited one of the Whitelands customers and it transpires that he is being investigated by the South Yorkshire Police.'

'On our patch! Kind of them to let us know, I feel bound to say.'

'Not on our patch, skipper. He lives in our patch but his suspect activities appear to be confined to Sheffield, where he works.'

'I see.'

'Chap called Braithwaite, a man of few words, is the interested officer in Sheffield. Said he'd clear it with us if they do anything on our patch.'

'Good.'

'But this fellow, Thornton by name, remembers who he gave the bag to. I traced the bag to his brother who runs an off sales in Holgate, who reuses plastic bags that his customers give him.'

'And thereafter?'

'Well, thereafter the trail went cold. The off sales proprietor couldn't remember which customer he gave the bag to or when he used it.'

Hennessey sat back in his chair. 'You see, Yellich, you have just proved my point. The only reason that man remembered to whom he gave the bag is because he gave it to his brother. It's the sort of thing you would remember and thereafter the trail, as you say, went cold. It is more than a fanciful line of inquiry, it's fruitless. So abandon it.'

'Very good, sir.'

'But thanks for suggesting it. Before you came in, I was pondering action.'

'Yes, boss.'

'I'd like you to go to the dentist's.'

'Oh . . .' Yellich flinched. 'You know, sir, I have never had a bad experience at the dentist's, not one, yet each time I cross the threshold of my dentist, I do so with trepidation. It's something to do with the drill on the enamel and it being inside your head . . .'

'Well this won't cause you trepidation. On Gillygate there is a dentist yclept Wheatman. He is the dentist whom Henry Fulwood saw for his dental treatment.'

'Yes, sir.'

'Can you obtain his dental records and convey them to Wetherby, where Henry Fulwood's skull now resides?'

'At the forensic science laboratory? Yes, sir.'

'Confirm that the skull is that of Henry Fulwood, then return the records to Mr Wheatman.'

'Sure thing, boss.'

'Mrs Fulwood, his ageing mother, gave good information. I offered to confirm the identity of the skull as being that of her son, it's something I'd like us to be able to do. The poor, good woman wanted a whole corpse to bury. All she has is a skull. Ponder attending a funeral, knowing only a skull is in the coffin . . .'

'Hardly bears thinking about.' Yellich shuddered.

'Doesn't, does it? But I said we would do that for her. If you could attend to that?'

'And confirm the identity to Mrs Fulwood?'

'Yes ... the whole business, please. I'm going to his last place of work.'

'Henry ... aye ... of course I remember him.' The manager of Yorkshire Dairies was a tall, slim man, grey suited, bespectacled, dark hair. He kept a neat desk. A hugely enlarged aerial photograph of the premises of Yorkshire Dairies hung in a wooden frame on the wall behind him. 'I remember him not so much as a worker, but because of the way he disappeared. Strange that ... very strange ... frightening.' His nameplate on his desk was M. Oliver B.A.(Hons).

'Utterly terrifying. It reached me for some reason.' Hennessey rested his elbows on the arms of the chair in which he sat, modern upholstered office furniture. 'The issue of missing people reaches me on a personal level, not just as a police officer.'

'Why ... have you ... ?'

'No, fortunately.' Hennessey anticipated Oliver's question. 'I have had my bereavements in life, as we all have, but I have always been able to bury or cremate my loved ones ... a funeral brings a closure, and it's a public statement, it allows one to move on in life ... but if a loved one just doesn't come home ... for days ... for weeks ... and the months turn into years ...'

'Torture.'

'Oh, yes ... so, Mr Fulwood?'

'A good, steady worker, quietly efficient, never caused any problems but he didn't work hard on his round. That's why I only really remember him because of the mystery of his disappearance. He was just a member of the crew and if he had moved on to pastures new, I would have difficulty recalling him. My brother-in-law is a teacher and he says of his pupils that you remember the good ones and you remember the bad ones, but many just don't make any impression on you and you rapidly forget them once they have left school, and it's like that here or in any large operation. You remember the good employees and you remember the bad ones, but many don't make any impression at all.'

'And Henry Fulwood was like that?'

'Yes ... he wasn't a management problem, though I would have liked him to have worked harder on his round, but he was happy just delivering milk.'

'Work harder? You mean more speedily?'

'Not necessarily, we sell cheese and eggs and yoghurt from the floats and we got the milkmen to ask their customers if they would buy products like that as well as the milk. Our prices are reasonable and of course, they are delivered. One or two milkmen must have really pestered their customers because they sold many cartons of eggs and such like ... earned themselves a bit of commission.'

'But not Henry?'

'Nope, ambled through his round, ambled to the pub on Friday evenings ... we collect on Fridays. The crew starts work at five a.m. and finish about ten p.m. ... walk across the road to the George and Dragon for a pint or two before going home. It's a long day for them.'

'I'll say.'

'Saw him ambling home the day before he was reported missing, giving directions, it seemed, to a man in a white van.'

'Sorry?' Hennessey raised his eyebrows. 'That was the day before he was reported missing?'

'Yes,' Oliver shrugged, 'is it significant?'

'You didn't think of mentioning it?'

'No, should I have done?'

It was, Hennessey thought, a fair point. 'Well perhaps in hindsight, you should have, but only in hindsight.'

'Thank you for saying that. So why the sudden interest in ambling Henry Fulwood?'

'Well, you will have read about the "Bag of Bones" case?'

'Yes . . . following it avidly, all England is I'll be bound.'

'Well, there's no reason why you shouldn't know this . . . we have informed the next of kin, but the skull among the bones was that . . .'

'Of Henry Fulwood?' Oliver gasped.

'Yes . . . but I would ask you to keep that under your hat, Mr Oliver.'

'Of course, as much as I can.'

'We will probably be disclosing his identity, it might encourage some to come forward, but the sighting of Henry giving directions to a man in a white van now becomes significant.'

'Yes, I can see that.'

'So . . . tell me about the white van.'

'It's some years ago now, Mr Hennessey.'

'Anything you can remember.'

'Well, there was no writing on the side, that I do remember because at the time a family friend who's been made redundant was trying to make a living as a man with a van. You know the type, small-scale removals, some-times just a single item of furniture that someone wants transported from A to B. The van was identical, a Ford Transit with a long wheelbase.'

'Ah, yes.'

'So as I drove past, I looked to see if it was Cyrus, but it wasn't. Cyrus had writing on the side of his vehicle.'

'I see. And you say Henry Fulwood was giving direc-tions?'

'Seemed to be . . . chatting and pointing with his hand. Just the gestures you'd use if giving directions.'

'Yes.'

'Well, I drove up from behind, so as I passed the driver was leaning away from me, talking to Henry, so I didn't see him.'

'But it was Henry Fulwood talking to the driver?'

'Most definitely.' Oliver stroked his smoothly shaven chin and glanced out of his office window. The view Hennessey saw was not all unpleasant. The dairy beneath the window, the empty loading bays, the stacks of crates containing empty bottles, metal crates containing nothing at all. Beyond the dairy were the rooftops of suburban York and beyond that, the green and brown of the winter Vale landscape, all under a vast and still near cloudless blue sky. 'Trying to think if I can remember anything that might help you. Like I said, Henry was one of those employees you don't remember. I don't think he had a special friend as such among the crew. He seemed to keep himself to himself, except on Fridays when he went for a beer for the hour before last orders were called.'

'That's after the long day?'

'Yes. The staff turnover here is very low, we have delivery men and women who have been working for twenty years, the same round for twenty years, and so many will remember Henry. They're all out at the moment, that's why the loading bays are empty. But if you wish to return, I am sure they'll be willing to give you what assistance they can.'

'I'll probably do that.'

'Lunchtime would be a good time. They're mostly all back by then and in the canteen, have a sandwich and a cup of tea. I'll ask the foreman to put the word round amongst the crew.'

'If you could, that would be very helpful. We understand he had a lady friend at the time of his disappearance? You wouldn't happen to know anything of her?'

'Not a thing, sorry, but again, one of the crew might.'

'Well thanks anyway, the white Ford Transit van might be useful, very useful indeed.' Hennessey stood. 'Where's the George and Dragon pub? It's near here, I believe?'

'Ten minutes' walk that way . . .' Oliver pointed away from the centre of York, 'fifteen minutes, at the most.'

'Do you mind if I leave my car in your car park, if I am to return to chat to the delivery men and women?'

'Not at all.' Oliver also stood. He was taller than Hennessey. 'In fact, I'll go down with you, introduce you to Mr Lane, the foreman.'

'Aye, I remember Henry Fulwood, he used to pop in here early doors.' The publican of the George and Dragon was a broad-shouldered, bald-headed individual; warm blue eyes, Hennessey thought, very warm. He spoke with a soft but very distinct Yorkshire accent. 'He was a milkman at the dairy down the road. He disappeared some years ago now, it was the talk of the pub at the time. Why the sudden interest, has he turned up?'

'In a sense.' Hennessey glanced round about him. The George and Dragon had its battery of electronic gambling machines and a jukebox, both mercifully silent at the moment, and television sets mounted on the wall at intervals around the room and above and behind the bar, but a large amount of the original pub seemed to Hennessey to have been preserved. The furniture was old and solid, the wood panelling on the wall seemed original. The George and Dragon had only just opened for the day's trade by the time Hennessey arrived, and it smelled of air freshener and furniture polish. A woman in a pink bonnet sat alone in the corner of the pub. A large schooner of sherry stood on the table in front of her.

'That's Gertie.' The publican followed Hennessey's gaze. 'She comes in each day when we open, has three schooners of sherry, starts talking to herself on the second one and starts singing on the third one and then leaves to sleep it off at home. It would be cheaper for her to buy a bottle and stay in. But it's all trade, all good custom and who can afford to turn away business?'

'Not many, that's for sure.'

'It's the need to get out of the house, I suppose.' The publican wiped the highly polished surface of the bar. 'Alcohol from off sales is always cheaper than in a pub, but it's the atmosphere of a pub, the chance of getting into a conversation, getting out of the house, but not walking the streets, a home from home. That's what a pub is. So Gertie and her likes can escape from whatever they're escaping from for an hour.'

'Aye . . . but Henry Fulwood?'

'Yes . . . he must have turned up, and turned up dead.'

'You think so?' Hennessey smiled.

'Well, has to be,' the publican returned the smile as he continued to wipe the surface of the bar. 'Otherwise you wouldn't be here asking about him. Would you?'

'Fair point, and yes, he has turned up, at least a bit of him has.'

'The bag of bones?' The publican stopped wiping the table. 'You are not going to tell me . . . ?'

''Fraid so.' Hennessey fixed the publican with a serious expression. The brief smile of earlier had gone. 'We'll be announcing it to the media soon, much to the distress of his family and friends, but we are certain that the skull among the bones is that of Henry Fulwood.'

'My . . . just the skull . . . of course it would be, the *Yorkshire Post* this morning, the article in there said the twelve bones were twelve different people.'

'Yes, they are. DNA tests confirmed it. But Henry

Fulwood is the only one to be identified, so we think that
if we investigate his murder, it will lead to the murderer
of all twelve.'

'Or murderers.'

'Indeed. So is there anything you can tell us, anything
at all? We understand he had a lady friend, for example.'

'Georgina . . . yes . . . though he wouldn't recognize her
now.'

'No?'

'No. Well, she could sink a good bucket could
Georgina, drank more than Henry did but since Henry
disappeared, she's really hit it hard. I don't mean hitting
it, I mean hitting it. She took Henry's disappearance
very badly.'

'I see. Where would I find Georgina?'

'At the church across the road.'

'The church?'

'Yes, she's the cleaner, caretaker, person on the premises at night. The Nonconformist church, red brick, can't
miss it. Folk here think it's a bit rich that strict teetotallers
like them have an alcoholic caretaker. But this is Yorkshire.
Strange things happen in the county and it's true . . .
there's nowt so queer as folk.'

'I'll nip over there.'

'This is a good time to find her half sober. Much later
and she'll be on her high horse about some injustice or
other she has suffered in life. And once she's on that high
horse, you'll never get her off it.'

'I see. I understand that Henry Fulwood had other friends
in the pub?'

'Who told you that!'

'His mother.'

'His mother? Hard to imagine Henry having a mother
who's still alive.'

'She's elderly, but nothing wrong with her brains. She

told me he used to come down here each day to drink with his friends.'

The publican exhaled. 'Well, listen, my good mate, I can tell you that if she said that, she's assuming it or Henry told her he had mates in the pub so she wouldn't think he was a lone bird.'

'But he was?'

'Yes. When he wasn't sitting with Georgina, he was standing at the bar, just him. And when he was with Georgina they were just the two of them. Two lone birds, together. Made a strange couple. Henry so big and rangy with a large north of England face, her so small and older than Henry. Henry was in his forties when he disappeared, I believe?'

'Yes.'

'Well, Georgina was a lot older . . . late fifties then . . . she'll be turned sixty now. They made an odd couple.' The man seemed to cast his mind back. 'Aye, she was the drinker. He didn't drink much. She was the smoker, he didn't smoke at all. It was all skew-whiff with those two . . . the older one, the hard drinker and the heavy smoker and the one who did the most talking was the woman. The demure one was the fella.'

'A white van. Know anything of one such vehicle in connection with Henry?'

'Sorry?'

'About the time that Henry Fulwood disappeared, he was seen talking to someone in a white van out on Haxby Road there.' Hennessey nodded to the door of the George and Dragon. 'He might have been giving directions, he might equally have been talking to someone to whom he was acquainted.'

'Well I don't . . . I'll ask in here for you, but like I said, they kept themselves well to themselves, hardly ever talked to anyone else, even in passing.'

'Thanks, anyway.' Hennessey left the George and Dragon and crossed Haxby Road and entered the grounds of the Nonconformist church. It was a large, rambling, late nineteenth-century building, all corners and turrets and roofs at varying angles. It had, noted Hennessey, the jagged roofline beloved of the Victorians. He walked around the outside of the building, allowing his feet to crunch the gravel so as to announce his presence. It did not at all do, he firmly believed, to creep quietly upon someone. He came upon a door marked 'Flat' at the rear of the building. He knocked on it. A dog barked from within.

The door was opened soon after he had knocked upon it, as if the occupant had been standing immediately behind it. The occupant revealed herself to be a small, finely built woman who wore a shabby fur coat and matching hat, painfully thin legs, clad only in nylon, finished with small boots which just covered her ankles. She had a thin, pointed face and bleered at Hennessey with bulging and blood-shot eyes. The fingers of her left hand gripped a 'roll-up' cigarette which seemed, to Hennessey, to have been smoked about halfway down its length.

'Georgina?' Hennessey took his ID from his jacket pocket.

'Aye.' The woman blinked as she read the ID card. 'Police? What's wrong?'

'I was hoping you could help us?'

'Us? Is there more of you?' She glanced behind Hennessey.

'Oh, quite a few,' Hennessey smiled. 'Quite a few . . . quite a few thousand, nationally speaking . . . quite a few hundred at Micklegate Bar, which is where I am based, but there's only me at your door.'

'Oh.'

'The landlord of the George and Dragon suggested I

call on you. He told me where to find you.'

'Oh yes . . . this is where I live.' She seemed, to Hennessey, to be about sixty and much wasted with drink and possibly tobacco as well.

'It's about Henry,' Hennessey spoke softly, 'Henry Fulwood. I gather you knew each other? I understand you were quite close in fact?'

'Henry . . .' Georgina's voice cracked. 'Oh, Henry . . . yes.'

'Can I come in?'

'That flat's a mess. I have been told to clean it up or I am getting evicted.'

'That's alright, I am a police officer, I have seen the inside of many houses . . . some you wouldn't believe.'

'Well, you might not believe this one, but come in anyway.' She turned and walked into her flat. Hennessey followed, stooping as he did so to get through the door-frame, which was unusually small, in his view, for a Victorian building. Inside, he had no difficulty seeing why Georgina had been told to clean up the flat. The smell almost overwhelmed Hennessey and seemed to come in the main from an old dog which lay on a settee. The dog was a long-haired mongrel, decaying with age, who was able to bark, just, but the days when he would run yapping or growling at strangers who entered his domain were clearly long past. The dog eyed Hennessey but made no sound at all. The flat was cold, very cold, so cold that Hennessey's breath condensed a little as he exhaled. He reflected that on a warm day in summer the stench of the flat would be difficult for a visitor to tolerate. He glanced round the room. Nothing seemed to be in its place, clothing lay strewn about and unwashed plates lay on the floor amid foil cartons which had once contained Chinese takeaway meals. The ashtray near the fire grate overflowed with ash and dog ends, and the grate itself was a receptacle for anything combustible. The kitchen and the toilet were places Hennessey did not wish to see.

Georgina walked with rapid steps to a chair near the fire and turned and sat on it. She suggested to Hennessey that he might sit next to the dog on the couch. Hennessey said thank you, but he'd prefer to stand.

'Don't blame you.' She flicked ash from her roll-up on to the ashtray. 'I told you it needed tidying.'

'Have you no heat?' Hennessey noticed a central-heating radiator under the window.

'No . . . heating hasn't worked for donkey's years. I wear the coat to keep warm and when I have enough stuff that burns in the fire grate, I set fire to it. It'll burn for a few minutes, 'cos it's mostly paper.'

'Don't you go out faggotting? Confess I would, if I were you.'

'Faggotting?'

'Collecting faggotts . . . small twigs that always lie about in fields and woodland, plenty this time of year blown from the trees. You just need a basket . . . get you out as well . . . it's really quite stuffy in here. You might be used to it, Georgina, but it really isn't healthy.'

'That's what they say.' She nodded at the wall. Hennessey assumed that she nodded in the direction of the minister's office. 'I've got a week to clean it up or I am out on my ear . . . me and Toby.'

At the mention of his name, the old dog looked at Georgina and managed a brief wag of his tail.

'Seems fair.'

'Well, I have been given a week to get it cleaned up before, and the deadline has come and gone. You see, they know if they evict me they won't get anybody else to live here, not in an unheated flat, just this one room to live and sleep in, a toilet, a little kitchen and no bath or shower.'

'No shower even?'

'No. I have a strip wash each day at the sink in the kitchen using water boiled in a kettle. It's how I have lived for years. They pay less than the Social would, but throw in this flat – it keeps the building occupied, someone on the premises each day and night. I am allowed to come and go as I please, but they like me to remain in more than out, especially at night. They're worried about getting their windows turned. Don't know why, there's nothing to steal, it's not like an old church with valuable communion goblets and such like.'

'I see.'

'But you want to talk about Henry?'

'Yes. Thank you for getting the conversation back on track, I shouldn't have let it wander.'

'Well, believe it or not, I used to be a nurse, still am in the sense I have the qualifications, but we were told that if we have to talk to a patient about something, it's best not to jump straight in. What was the word they used? A rapport . . . build up a rapport, then tell them how to change their colostomy bag . . . and you thought you had a dirty job.' She smiled. 'So you built up a rapport.'

Hennessey took his notebook from his pocket. 'Could you tell me your surname please?'

'Tew. Georgina Tew.'

'Do you prefer Georgina or Miss or Mrs Tew?'

'Georgina's fine.' She drew heavily on the cigarette then flicked the end towards the fire grate.

'So, Henry Fulwood . . . a good friend of yours?'

'Was. There was some age gap between us but we just clicked. He didn't mind me drinking like I do and did then. About the only man that didn't. Men can be so two-faced, they get legless and think it's clever and funny but don't like women to drink . . . but Henry wasn't like that, he didn't care when old Georgina had a drink, and a good drink. Liked him for that.'

69

'Can you remember when he disappeared?'

'Very well. Old Georgina's old life stopped then. No partner at all. Not since, but nobody could fill Henry's part, so big and so gentle.'

'Did he have many friends?'

'Henry . . . no.' Georgina shook her head slowly. 'He was a bit of a loner . . . he had me, I had him. There was just the two of us.'

'What about enemies? Anybody that would want to do him harm?'

'Don't think so . . .'

'You sound uncertain.'

'Well, about the time he disappeared he was getting hassle.'

'Hassle? What sort?'

'Fella on the estate he delivered to, not the estate he lived on, but Huntingdon.'

'Yes, my sergeant lives there.'

'Well, there was a guy on the Huntingdon estate kept picking fights with him.'

'Do you know what it was about?'

'Money, I think. This guy reckons that Henry made some comment about the guy's wife not being a good house-keeper, never able to pay her milk money each Friday, or paying a bit off each week.'

'What was Henry's version?'

'Said it was true about the woman's ability to budget, but he never commented, more than his job was worth, Yorkshire Dairies is strong on customer relations, always wants its "milkies" to be ever so polite at all times. Henry also said that the guy never went to the dairy with the complaint, but just wanted to pick a fight with Henry each time they met. Even drove his van at him once . . . tried to run him down.'

'His van?'

'Guy had a van.'

'Really? What colour?'

'Colour? White. Saw him once, was walking to the pub with lovely Henry and a van went past with the driver pumping the horn. Henry said, "That's the guy that's been giving me grief."'

'Did you see the driver?'

'No, he was driving away from us by then.'

'But he lived on the Huntingdon estate at the time Henry disappeared?'

'So Henry said.'

'That's very interesting, Georgina. Thank you.'

'Why the sudden interest?'

George Hennessey told her and left her when he realized she was inconsolable and just needed space, an awful lot of space.

Yellich saw what Hennessey meant about Mrs Fulwood: frail, elderly, but with a strong and alert mind, and a strong emotional constitution as well. She seemed to smile, which puzzled Yellich, until he realized he was witnessing a grimace, the two expressions being similar by sight but conveying wholly different emotions. 'So it is our Henry?'

'I'm afraid so, Mrs Fulwood. There's no mistake. The dental records are a perfect match.'

'I see. I'm glad his father isn't alive to see this . . . to have this happen. I will have to go and see a priest . . . I don't know what to say. I am not a churchgoer and never have been, but how do you bury a head, just a head?'

Yellich remained silent. He struggled for something to say. The clock's ticking seemed louder, the room smaller and more cluttered, as he keenly felt the awkwardness of the situation. Then he said, 'I don't think we can release the . . . the . . .' He struggled to find the appropriate word.

'The skull,' Mrs Fulwood rescued him. 'It's my son's skull . . . my Henry's skull, his head . . . just call a spade a bloody shovel and have done with it.'

'Thanks . . . well, I don't think we can release Henry's remains.'

'Such as they are.'

'If you like . . . his remains yet, anyway, but I would be inclined to wait until this investigation is over. The bag of bones was clearly left for someone to find and report the find to the police . . . the rest of the remains might be there to be found . . . out there somewhere. While that possibility remains . . .'

'Yes . . . aye . . . that's good advice, lad. I'll take my time. See what comes out in the wash.'

George Hennessey returned to the dairy, turning his coat collar up against the blustery easterly as he walked down Haxby Road. At the dairy, Freddie Lane, a stocky man with short dark hair and, Hennessey found, a warm manner and steady look in his eyes, had questioned the milkmen and women as they had returned from their rounds. Many had by then gone home though a few remained in the canteen in case Hennessey would like to question them, but none had indicated to the foreman that they could shed any light on Henry Fulwood's disappearance.

'Did Henry ever mention anything to you about a difficult customer on his round?'

'Not to me, Mr Hennessey, but I'll ask around for you.'

'If you could, I'd appreciate it . . . married man on the Huntingdon estate, drove a white van.'

'A white van? Mr Oliver and I were chatting after you left, he mentioned seeing Henry talking to a fellow in a white van on the day he disappeared.'

'Yes. So he said. It's necessary to trace that man if we

can. He's suddenly become very germane to this inquiry. Is Mr Oliver in his office?'

'I believe he is.'

Hennessey went to Michael Oliver's office. Oliver listened attentively to Hennessey and then said, 'Yes . . . yes . . . they may not have been gestures of giving directions, they could easily have been gestures of anger as in an argument. Yes indeed.'

Man or woman? That was the man's question. He waited in the car, a Volvo estate, fifteen years old, black, no hubcaps, nothing shiny . . . just black, all black like the New Zealand rugby team, all black, all black, to hide in the night . . . the night is good for hiding in. The man liked the night. Man or woman? Women are easier, not as strong, and easier to scare, but the man, the one man he had abducted, he was a challenge: placid, very placid, took a lot to provoke him, but he eventually rose to the provocation, took the bait, came close enough to get a blast of Mace in the face, slumped, got bundled into the van in broad daylight . . . broad daylight . . . got trussed up, gagged and driven to the farm as the others had been down the years, and as the others had been down the years, kept alive . . . for company . . . and interesting company he had been, a merchant seaman for many years, a strong man, plenty of muscle, he lived for nearly six weeks before starvation took him . . . all the water he could drink, but no food. He enjoyed eating meals in his company, that longing look in his eyes, how he longed for a scrap of meat that was dropped on the floor . . . just out of his reach, but 3/8ths chain is strong stuff, too strong even for a merchant seaman, especially one who is getting weaker by the day. Then he 'croaked' as his American cousin would say, the cousin who visited occasionally and kindly supplied the Mace, so very useful and not obtainable in the UK.

The wait began, when after he had 'croaked', the man loved that word 'croaked' – his cousin had such a punchy way of talking, as when describing a man being 'creamed' by a machine gun – the wait until the blood in his body solidified. Murdering someone is easy, it's the easiest thing in the world to take human life; the difficulty is disposing of the corpse. Especially if you live in a crowded island like Britain . . . those Aussies . . . that outback . . . just drive out of the city, turn off the road for a few yards, toss the thing out and no one will find it, but here in the right little, tight little island, it's not that easy, so when the victim has croaked there's a waiting period . . . forty-eight hours . . . twenty-four would do it, but the man always waited for another twenty-four hours on top – no one came near the farm anyway. Then, when the blood was guaranteed dry, the body could be sawn up, a little bit saved for the trophy bag, and the rest burnt on a bonfire on the farm. What's so strange about that, especially when the farmer is standing next to it 'poking' it occasionally? No member of the public nearer than 200 yards, and then in cars, driving by. Few walked to the grass verge, very few. Then the bones were put in a pit, covered over and a tree planted . . . twelve trees so far, twelve apple trees, cookers and eaters . . . blossoming so sweetly each spring, nourished by the charred flesh and bones around which their roots must be lovingly wrapping themselves, and a trophy from each, kept . . . Now victim number thirteen is needed, wanted, desired . . . the game is notched up because the police now know he exists, soon they will know another one has been abducted, they'll know because he will tell them and he will tell them that he or she is being starved to death. Catch me if you can before the victim dies a horrible, horrible, agonizing death . . . The body eats itself and the pain is all over

74

and cancer-like in its intensity – so it seemed to the man as he observed his victims in the later stages, in their last week or two of life.

So man or woman? The man had been more difficult but more challenging – the success was sweeter because of it . . . Less sense of achievement with the women. Much less. Too easily overcome, and they didn't last as long as the man: one went in just three weeks, so she got a cooking-apple tree on top of her bones, but the man was rewarded with a lovely eating-apple tree. Fair play. So a challenge or an easy ride?

In the event, the decision was made for him. As soon as he saw her, he knew she was the one. He knew she was number thirteen. Even though she was pleasantly slender and so wouldn't last long . . . another three-weeker . . . even so, even despite that, he knew he just had to have her.

Later the man drove home. Behind him in the rear passenger footwell was number thirteen. As he drove he went over the abduction in his head: sitting in the car on a quiet road, a few houses about but not near, the real danger had been the possibility of another motorist passing by, but the man took risks, he enjoyed taking risks – it was all part of the game, all part of the thrill. The woman was on foot, she was in her twenties, he thought, late twenties, maybe even early thirties, and as she approached even closer, he put her age at mid to late thirties. She had held her figure well, still slender, but worry lines on her face betrayed her age. Her age also explained why she was walking confidently along a quiet semi-rural road, despite being alone, so the man reasoned: simply because she thought she was no longer of interest to predatory males. How wrong you are, he thought, how wrong you are. As she neared, he got out of the car and approached, holding a map. He smiled and said, 'Excuse me. Could you help me, please? I am confused by this map.' She had smiled a smile which was a mixture of politely wishing to help and of curiosity. She'd turned to the man and said, 'Where do you want to go?' But what sealed her fate was that she wasn't wearing spectacles: contact lenses won't protect you against Mace but spectacles will. The map concealed the spray can with its pistol grip. He lifted the can and sprayed the irritant into her eyes. She gasped and lowered her head – when something's in a person's eye, he or she will put their head down – and number thirteen was no different. Down went her head, and down came the man's fist on the back of her neck, and as she crumbled unconscious to the ground, he lifted her up and bundled her into the car; laid her in the footwell, threw a blanket over her and drove home, back to the farm. They hadn't all been as easy as that: the man, for instance, had to be clubbed with the wooden handle before he went down.

The woman started to moan softly as he turned off the road and up the drive to his house. She would take some time to come round fully and that, he believed, was in his interest. She could be walked, while still groggy, to the room – it would be easier than carrying her and she would be docile and easily handled.

Two hours later, as the winter sun sank in a fierce red ball behind leafless trees, the woman had fully regained consciousness. She had pulled at the chain which fastened her ankle to the wall and had come to glare angrily at the man. She showed no fear. Just anger, a lot of anger. The man thought she must be a tyrant to live with, dominating her household, getting what she wants the instant she wants it. It had always astounded the man that such women actually find husbands.

'Linda Handy.' The man read the credit card he had taken from the woman's wallet, which she wore round her neck on a slender chain.

'That's my purse!' the woman snapped. 'Give it to me.'

'No,' the man smiled, 'you're wrong . . . it's not your purse . . . it's mine.'

'I'll scream.'

'Okay.' The man emptied the contents of the purse on the table. 'This is a farm, there's no one here but me. And you. No one can hear you.'

Linda Handy glared at him.

'It's a good job for you that you're out of reach.'

The man turned and smiled. 'No,' he said quietly, 'it's a good job for you that you are out of reach.'

The woman sank back against the wall. 'So how long are you going to keep me here?'

The man shrugged. 'Well . . . that depends.'

'We are not rich. My husband is a salesman in farming equipment.'

'Good for him!'

'He won't be able to raise any sort of ransom.'

'I don't want any sort of ransom.'

'So, what do you want?'

'A game.'

'What sort of game?'

The man didn't reply. He stood and left the room. He returned one hour later, carrying a warm and substantial meal on a tray. He ate in silence, watched in equal silence by the woman. He forked the last mouthful into his mouth and dropped the fork contemptuously on to the plate.

The woman seethed with indignation, but remembering her training, she spoke softly. 'Don't you feed your prisoners?'

'No,' the man smiled, 'I don't. That's the answer to your question. That's the game I want to play. They've got to find you before you starve to death. I'll give you a plastic bucket in which to do your functions, and I'll empty and clean it each day. And each morning I'll give you a bowl of hot water and a bar of soap and I'll leave you so you can strip wash. I will give you as much water as you want to drink. But no food. You won't be my first victim.' He enjoyed seeing the look of terror creep into the woman's eyes and thought: Not so much of a tyrant now, are you? 'You know the bag of bones case, it's been big news in the last day or two?'

'Yes . . .' The woman's voice cracked. 'You . . . ?'

'Yes . . . me. It's a horrible death. Very painful. I read that your body eats itself. The man lasted five weeks . . . just there where you are now.'

'There were bones of twelve different people in that shopping bag.'

'Yes –' again he smiled – 'the rest of them are outside in the ground. That's why I like living on a farm. You can do more than you can in the city. I grew up in a little terraced house in the city. Couldn't do this in a terraced house in the town.' He stood. 'I have to leave you . . . I work at night.'

'On a farm?'

But the man didn't reply.

Hennessey gripped the phone. He said nothing but listened intently . . . it was the same voice . . . faint . . . timid.

'I tried to stop him, he wouldn't listen . . . he never listens to little me . . . to Horace . . . that's me, but he'll be doing it again . . . soon, you've got to stop him.'

'Where do we find him?' Hennessey spoke softly.

'Can't tell you.'

The phone was put down hurriedly. Hennessey replaced his own receiver. He glanced at Yellich. 'Second time that guy's phoned. Calls himself Horace . . . sounds young . . . teenager . . . he used a call box, heard traffic in the background. Just says "he" did it . . . and he couldn't stop him.'

'A crank?' Yellich pondered. 'Horace' rang a bell for him, but he couldn't place it – it seemed distant yet near at the some time. He decided not to mention it.

'I'm inclined to think so.'

Four

in which Hennessey makes a house call, and Somerled Yellich and family are at home to the gentle reader.

Hennessey sat forward, rested his elbow on his desk and cupped his jaw with his left palm. 'A white van on the Huntingdon estate.'

'Doesn't ring any bells with me, boss, but me and Sara have only been on the estate for four years. We could ask among our neighbours.'

'If you would. On estates like that, people get to know each other's cars, and it's a fairly settled estate, I believe?'

'Yes . . . you can say that. After a few years, we are still considered newcomers. People either side of us have been in their houses for about fifteen years. Some have been there since the estate was built.' Yellich sat back in his chair. 'Do you want me to get on to that now, do a house-to-house?'

'Yes . . . if you would.' Hennessey paused. 'It's the only thing we can do, the missing persons register can't help us . . . not enough information given by a bone alone, I would have thought.'

'Don't you think so, skipper?' Yellich raised his eyebrows.

'Why?' Hennessey looked at him. 'What do you suggest?'

'Well, have van will travel, so our boy could have trawled for his victims or abducted people who were passing through and so they would not be on our mis per register.'

'But . . .'

'Well, some might. We know that one of his victims was reported missing five years ago. We don't know when the last one was abducted but the flesh has completely rotted from the bone. In this climate that could take about two years.'

'Go on,' Hennessey smiled at him.

'We don't know when the first one was abducted but we could safely assume that it was less than twenty years ago.'

'Alright . . .'

'Probably nearer ten.'

'Again . . . go on.'

'Well, can I put it to you that well-built, or strong, or elderly people don't get abducted?'

'Fair enough . . . as a general rule.'

'So, if we look again at the missing persons register and identify people who by their profile seem likely abductees . . . we might be able to obtain their DNA. We could see if it matches any of the DNA we have obtained from the bones. Just a thought, boss.'

'And a good thought indeed.' Hennessey beamed at him, though inwardly he felt disappointed that he had not identified that avenue, and Commander Sharkey's anecdote of the unfortunate John Taighe, the out-of-his-depth teacher, rose spectre-like in his mind. 'Can you address that? Have to ask the uniformed branch to do a house-to-house on the estate.'

'I could just as easily ask our Sara . . . just a phone call.

She's well in with the neighbours, word of mouth round the estate will produce results as speedily as a house-to-house.'

'Probably speedier.' Hennessey grinned. 'Is there a post office on the estate?'

'No, there isn't.'

'Pity. That would be a place to ask.'

'Certainly would.' Yellich stood. 'I'll phone our Sara, then go through the mis per files. I'll go back ten years.'

'As you wish.'

Yellich left Hennessey's office, leaving Hennessey sitting alone, continuing to feel awkward and embarrassed that Yellich, not he, had thought of that initiative, that he had too easily dismissed the mis per register as a possible source of good information, apart from the skull. His phone rang. He snatched it up angrily. 'Yes!'

'Switchboard, sir.' The operator's voice was calm, deferential, efficient.

'Yes!'

'Gentleman on the line, sir, asked to speak to the officer in charge of the "Bag of Bones" case.'

'Put him through.' Hennessey calmed himself.

The line clicked. There was a silence. A weak-sounding, squeaky voice, in Hennessey's view, said, 'Hello?'

'Hello. DCI Hennessey.'

'My name is Grimshaw.'

'Yes, Mr Grimshaw?' He thought how appropriately did the name fit the voice.

'I have received a phone call. It has worried me.'

'Oh?' Instinctively Hennessey reached for his pen and notepad.

'I am the editor of the *Wirral Free Press* . . . We are a small free newspaper, exist on advertising revenue, and deliver to people's doors . . . you must know the type of paper.'

'Yes, we have a local version.'

'Well, just now I received a phone call from a man claiming to be responsible for the "Bag of Bones" murders . . . the case has received national publicity.'

'Yes.' Hennessey's brow furrowed.

'Well, he phoned me . . . at the newspaper. Mr Hennessey, he told me he had abducted number thirteen.'

A chill shot down Hennessey's spine. 'Why did he phone *you*?'

'What he said was that he picked our paper at random . . . a list of newspapers is not hard to obtain . . . we dialled 1471 as soon as he terminated his call but he had shielded his number.'

'I see.'

'He gave her name as . . . I wrote it down . . . Linda Handy. She's the wife of a salesman and has an address in Malton. He told me that he is going to starve her to death . . . like he did with the others.'

Hennessey swallowed hard.

'Did you get the impression he was serious?'

'Yes. Just intuitively . . . I felt he was serious. Insanely so.'

'What was his voice like?'

'Cold. Very cold. Yorkshire accent, but what part of Yorkshire, I couldn't tell. I read once that there were forty-four different Yorkshire accents . . . but being a Lancastrian, I can't tell the difference . . . well, maybe Sheffield and Leeds. In Sheffield I have heard a "coat" pronounced as "coo-at" and Leeds as "coy-it" . . . but that's as far as I can go. This fella just sounded Yorkshire.'

'Anything in the background?'

'Breakfast television . . . quite loud, as though he was trying to drown out any sound that might identify the location. I had to take the call seriously, it wasn't my place to dismiss it as a hoax.'

'Of course.'

'He said he would be contacting you again, but he would phone another journal, he would contact you via editors of small newspapers or magazines . . . but he said you would know it was him because he will use the code name "Dance Master" to identify himself.'

'Dance Master?'

'He said he's been leading the police a merry dance all these years . . . twelve victims . . . and now he has number thirteen. He says . . .'

'He says . . .' Hennessey echoed as he drew a circle round the words 'Dance Master' as he had written them on the pad.

'I'm afraid that that is the sum of what he said, Chief Inspector.'

'He didn't mention a ransom?'

'No . . . no, he didn't.'

'Well, thank you, Mr Grimshaw, thanks indeed.'

'Best of luck, sir.'

'Thank you.' Hennessey replaced the phone gently, muttered 'Dance Master' to himself and then picked up the phone again and tapped a four-figure internal number.

'Switchboard.'

'The police at Malton, please.' DCI Hennessey here.

'Yes, sir.'

Hennessey held the line, waiting to be put through.

'Police at Malton, PC Prenderghast speaking.'

'DCI Hennessey, Micklegate Bar Police Station.' He was impressed by Prenderghast's manner: it said young, conscientious, keen, like a man who was going to go far in the police.

'Do you know if a lady called Handy . . . Linda Handy has been reported missing?'

'Yes, sir . . . she has. I took a call from her husband shortly after nine this forenoon.' Prenderghast paused. 'I told him I couldn't accept a mis per report on an adult until twenty-four hours had elapsed since he or she was last seen, as per procedure.'

'Yes.'

'He became quite irate, quite convinced that some ill had befallen her . . . wanted us to search for her.'

'I think he has cause to be fearful.'

'Really, sir?'

'Yes, really. Do you have a note of his address?'

Prenderghast dictated it, clearly and slowly, then gave directions to it.

Hennessey drove slowly out of York, through New Earswick, and joined the A64, which he followed to Malton. The road was, to his mind, tolerably free of traffic; the vastness of the blue sky over the flatlands of the Vale of York was interspersed with high white clouds. Only the drabness of the landscape, the ploughed fields, the leafless trees, betrayed the fact that it was still winter. Perhaps another person might have enjoyed that short drive, but George Hennessey was a man possessed of demons, one of which set him apart from the majority of adult males in the Western world, a demon that made him loathe the internal combustion engine, and hate having to drive.

He halted his car at the approach to Malton and consulted the notes he had taken as PC Prenderghast had given directions to the Handy house. A few moments later he halted his car for a second time, this time on a quiet suburban street, outside a modest three-bedroom semi-detached house. 'This,' he said to himself, 'this will not be easy.'

Hennessey left his car and walked up the driveway to the front door and tapped the police officer's tap: *tap, tap* . . . *tap*. The door was opened swiftly by a tall, muscular man, casually dressed, and with a face lined with worry.

'Yes?' The man's voice had an urgency about it which Hennessey thought bordered on the desperate.

'Police.' He showed his ID.

'Oh . . .' The man jolted, and Hennessey, a people-watcher all his working life and a man who, over the years, had shown many times that he was possessed of a great deal of insight, had the immediate and strong impression that, despite his physical appearance, this man was weak within and very wife-dependent. 'What? Where's Linda?'

'Can I come in please, Mr Handy?'

The visit to Handy, the knowledge of the dread possibility that was about to unfold, caused Hennessey suddenly to recall his own loss, his own dear wife who had been so cruelly snatched from him, from their son, indeed from her own life and future and when aged only 23 years. He remembered it as clearly as any man would. He recalled that he had been mowing the front lawn of their house . . . A police car had pulled up at the kerb – there was nothing unusual in that, nothing unusual at all, except that this time there was no smile on the constable's face, no acknowledgement of Hennessey's hand raised in greeting. The constable's face had remained frozen in an expression of seriousness. He had approached Hennessey, clearly avoiding eye contact as he did so, and had suggested that it might be better if they could talk inside . . . Sitting at the kitchen table, Hennessey had been told as gently as possible of Jennifer's death . . . collapsed in the street . . . of how people had at first thought she had fainted . . . an ambulance was called but she was pronounced dead on arrival. There had been of course not just the shock but the disbelief: the refusal to accept such a thing could be true . . . what, later in life, he learned was the state of mind which psychologists called 'denial' . . . The thin thread of hope that a mistake as to her identity had been made evaporated when he was asked to identify her body, so young, so attractive, lying peacfully upon the stretcher behind the pane of glass ... yes, yes, it was she ... but so deathly white. Then there had been the difficult days of adjustment that followed, days of adjustment that could be measured in years: coping with their infant son – with hired help so as to allow Charles to remain at home and Hennessey to remain employed – carrying on alone when he had expected to be enjoying married bliss and shared parenting. Hennessey knew what Handy might well be going to experience. He knew the long and lonely years that might well be what was ahead of this man upon whose door he had unexpectantly knocked. Handy seemed shocked ... dazed. Hennessey asked a second time if he might enter the man's house.

'Yes, please, do come in. Sorry about the mess.'

The mess transpired to be children's toys scattered about the hallway and in the living room where Handy took Hennessey and invited him to take a seat. Hennessey sank into a deep armchair and commented that it wasn't a mess at all.

'They're at school, got them into some form of normality but they sense something is wrong ... wanting to know where Mummy is. The police in Malton said they can't take a missing persons report until she has been missing for twenty-four hours.'

'That's the procedure.' Hennessey glanced out of the windows into the back garden, where stood a climbing frame and a swing on the lawn. 'Most adults who go missing turn up within twenty-four hours and police time is stretched and limited.'

'Yes ... I dare say I can understand that.' Handy too sat in an armchair.

'To be honest, it wouldn't make a deal of difference,

taking a missing persons report just means we note details and attach a photograph, it doesn't mean to say we start searching for the missing person.'

'Yes . . . I work for a large organization, procedures for everything . . . works . . . seems to anyway, the whole machine turns over smoothly enough compared to other places I have lent my services.'

'What do you do, Mr Handy?'

'A salesman for D.F.R.'

'Ah, yes . . . I have seen the logo and the offices, never knew what the initials stood for.'

'Dalton's Farmers Requisites.'

'Really!'

'Yes, really . . . anything from a roll of chicken-wire to a combine harvester. You name it, if the farmer wants it, D.F.R. can supply it.'

'Well.'

'But you haven't called on me to chat about my employment?'

'No . . . it's about your wife, Mr Handy, and it's as well you are sitting down.'

'Oh . . . she's dead?'

'No . . . it's good news and it's bad news. There's no easy way of saying this, so I'll just say it. Your wife appears to have been kidnapped.'

'Kidnapped,' Handy gasped, 'but why Linda? I am not a rich man, I can't afford a ransom.'

'The kidnapper doesn't want a ransom. He's playing a game with us . . . but it's a deadly game.' And Hennessey explained the situation as carefully as he could, as clearly as he could, and as sensitively as he could. Handy listened with paling face and dropping jaw. 'So how long have we got?'

'Well, every second is critical. She's already been without her evening meal and breakfast . . . If the kidnapper is serious – and we have to assume he is – she'll be feeling quite hungry.'

'Ravenous, I'd say. She has a powerful appetite. She's very strong as well . . . physiologically speaking, I mean . . . mentally strong as well, she runs this house. What clues have you got?'

'None.' Hennessey eyed Handy with a grim stare. 'None. None at all. Which is the other reason for me being here.'

'But the man who called himself the "Dance Master", he knew that the bones of twelve people were found in that plastic bag?'

'And so does anyone who reads the newspapers or watches the television news . . . that tells us nothing.'

'Doesn't, does it . . . but starvation?' Handy looked at the carpet then at the mantelpiece. 'I have one of those eclectic minds, I receive and lodge all sorts of information, I just do, makes me very good at Trivial Pursuits. I read about starvation once . . . horrible.' He paused. 'And the newspaper received the call this morning?'

'Yes.'

'She could be anywhere in the UK. Abroad even.'

'Could be . . . but the man had a local accent.'

'Still could be anywhere, and it doesn't mean his ordinary, everyday speaking voice is that of a Yorkshire accent. I mean, you might hear the occasional trace of Yorkshire in my voice, I say "bath" not "barth" as the Southeners do . . . I speak of Sir Walter "Rally" not Sir Walter "Raarlie", again as a Southerner would, but I have had to cultivate as near a middle-class "received pronunciation" speaking voice as I could in order to progress as a salesman. People just won't buy a baling machine or tens of thousands of pounds worth of fertilizer from a salesman in a cloth cap who says, "Ayup, lad, ow's thee today?" But the fact is that I grew up in this town, went to the council

school here and I can speak in a Yorkshire accent when-
ever I wish to.'

'Point taken,' Hennessey inclined his head, 'but
somehow I don't think he is trying to put us off the scent.
We will be taking advice from a forensic psychologist,
but as I said to my sergeant the other day, I think he wants
to be caught.'

'Yes . . . I've also read of such men.' Handy sat back
in his chair. '"Catch me if you can" mentality, but they
stumble so as to be caught. I mean they deliberately stumble
because they can't just walk into a police station and give
themselves up.'

'That sort of person, yes. And for that reason, I don't
think that he is disguising his normal speaking voice . . .
but he's making it impossible to tape-record his voice
because he's contacting us through newspapers but using
a code word.'

'Like the IRA used to do during the Troubles? No direct
voice contact with the authorities, who may, just may, be
taping all incoming calls.'

'Exactly. So we won't be able to ask the media to broad-
cast his voice . . . unless he stumbles, that won't be for a
while, puts pressure on us. I also think he's local and
holding your wife locally because the bag of bones was
placed locally and one of the victims was a local man.
We also have a lead involving a white van which is believed
to be owned locally.'

'I see . . . all roads are leading to Rome.'

'Seems so. So when did you last see your wife?'

'Yesterday lunchtime.'

'You are not working this week?'

'No, I have leave to use up. If I don't take it before the
end of March I lose it. So I took these five days off . . .
just pottering about the house. Up until yesterday I was
discovering it was more relaxing than going on a holiday

. . . the stress of late flights, strange foods . . . my eclectic mind also remembers reading that the most relaxing holiday is just to stay at home among familiar surroundings and I was indeed finding that to be the case.'

'Good job you are here, though, for the children.'

'You think so?' Handy fixed Hennessey with a steely glare. 'The only reason Linda went out was because I'd be here for when the children returned home from school. If I had been at work, she wouldn't have been abducted.'

'Sorry . . . crass of me . . . but you mustn't blame yourself.'

'Well, I can't help not to.'

'So, where did your wife go when she left the house?'

'To the stables. I have walked the route and now you have told me what you have told me, there is something I want to show you.'

'Oh, what?'

'Well, see what you think.'

Noel Handy led Hennessey from his house, turning right, and away from the centre of Malton. Hennessey found Handy to be a strong, fast walker, but was able to keep up with him. Within five minutes of leaving the Handy household, they were at the edge of the built-up area of Malton and edging out into the country.

'Not much further,' Handy said. It was the only time he spoke during the walk.

'Good, it's getting to be a car drive distance.'

The two men walked on side by side along a grassed-over verge until Handy stopped and pointed to the ground. 'There.'

The verge where Handy pointed was scored with the tyre tracks of a vehicle and indentation of footprints.

'Any colder or warmer and those marks wouldn't be there.' Handy spoke matter of factly. 'But this is where Linda was abducted.'

91

'You know that?'

'Yes. Intuitively. She had gone to the stables. This is the route she took, ironically believing it to be safer than taking the direct route across the fields. I walked to the stables yesterday, to find out where she was. I left the children with a neighbour, it was getting dark, but light enough to see. I thought nothing of them but just now, when you told me she had been abducted, it was then, then that I knew the significance of these marks.'

Hennessey plunged his hand into his jacket pocket and extracted his mobile phone. 'Hate these things, but there's no doubting their use, especially at times like this.' He pressed a series of numbers and held the phone to his ear. 'Can't take a railway journey without hearing one half of a conversation . . . Come on . . . come on. Yes, hello, DCI Hennessey, I want a CSE team at this location. It is . . .' Hennessey looked at Handy. 'Where does this road lead?'

'To Coneysthorpe.'

'From Malton . . . take the Coneysthorpe road and drive until you see me. We need casts and photographs of tyre and foot prints. Very good . . . as quick as you like, they're not as good as I'd like them to be but it's better than nothing. Right . . . thanks.'

Hennessey switched off the mobile and pocketed it. He glanced around him. One or two houses he saw were inter-visible with the abduction scene. They would have to be called on for form's sake though Hennessey privately held little hope that anyone would have seen anything, for the simple reason that unless they were brain-dead they would have reported a woman being overpowered and bundled into a car. At least he hoped they would.

'CSE?' Handy asked.

'Crime scene examiners.'

'So, how long have we got?'

'Well . . .' Louise D'Acre's voice was soft yet authoritative, 'the body will eat its reserves of fat for the first few days . . . then it wil begin to eat itself.'

'Eat itself!'

'Yes, it'll start chewing away at major organs depending on the strength and level of nourishment of the person . . . death will occur any time after two weeks . . . could take as long as six weeks . . . People can be nursed back to an apparent full recovery but they will succumb to organ failure in later life due to the damage done by starvation.'

'So . . . we've got a few days if we want to avoid permanent damage . . . a week or two if we want to avoid her dying of starvation.'

'Yes,' Louise D'Acre said quietly. 'That's about the size of it.'

'Many thanks.' Hennessey replaced his telephone receiver. 'Not a lot of time,' he said to himself. 'Not a lot of time at all.'

Hennessey sat in Yellich's office.

'One or two children, sadly –' Yellich looked over the list of names – 'but I eliminated them. It was clear from Dr D'Acre's report that all the bones were from adults.'

'Yes.'

'There are quite a few possible names. Twelve people, excluding Fulwood, who have been reported missing to us in the last ten years remain missing . . . A real tragedy for their families.'

'Aye.'

'And of course, they may be unconnected with the case. If our man has a car, and it seems he does . . . he could roam far and wide in search of his prey.'

'You'll be calling on each household anyway?'

'Yes, boss.'

'Well, I hope you have more luck than I did.'

'Oh, don't know, you got plaster casts and photographs of a possible crime scene.'

'No identifiable tread could be lifted, all the CSE boys could tell me was that the tyres were wide . . . a large vehicle.'

'Like a van?'

'Like a van, as you say.'

'Well, our Sara's done her bit, asked who she knows on the estate about the white van . . . the word is going round, I am sure we'll get a result.'

'Again, more than I got when I called on the houses that overlooked the abduction scene . . . if it was the abduction scene, though I tend to think Handy is correct . . . a cluster of footprints, male and possibly female, large and small, more or less facing each other . . . deeply indented heels, it's the sort of trace a struggle would produce.'

'So you did get something, boss.'

Hennessey smiled. 'I suppose . . . but not as much as I would have liked, but who ever does? Are you lunching in?'

'Yes, boss . . . up to the canteen for me, cheap and filling.'

'Which is all you can say for it.' Hennessey stood. 'I am going to lunch out.'

'Are you going public with the abduction of Linda Handy?'

'Have to. I'll prepare a press release after lunch.'

Hennessey signed out at the enquiry desk and walked out of the police station and joined the walls at Micklegate Bar. He walked the walls to Lendal Bridge, as indeed he had to, the walls of the ancient city being, unlike those of Chester, incomplete and surviving in three major sections. From Lendal Bridge he walked to Stonegate and turned into a snickelway, at the end of which was the entrance to Ye Olde Starre Inne, reputedly one of York's oldest pubs. He sat in a quiet corner under low beams – behind him on the wall was a framed reproduction of a 1610 map of 'The West Ridinge of Yorkshyre, with the moft famous and fayre Citie York defcribed'. He relished his meal of Cumberland sausage with onions and gravy, though he spared a thought for Linda Handy, whose hunger, if the 'Dance Master' was carrying out his threat, would be by then very noticeable indeed.

She sat against the wall, knees together, tucked under her chin, arms clasped round her legs, watching him eat. She had by then been without food for twenty-four hours; the pain in her stomach was intense. She told herself that it was only the pain of her stomach shrinking, that it didn't mean harm was being done to her body . . . that, she knew, would come later. What did worry her was the feeling of her strength being sapped, of feeling constantly faint. She glanced at the man, who occasionally held up a knife full of food for her to see before putting it in his mouth. She refused to react, refused to give him the satisfaction of seeing that his actions were having the desired effect.

'Hungry?'

'A little,' she conceded.

The man smiled. 'You're not. You might think you are. What's it been, about twenty-four hours? Wait till it's been a week. That's hunger . . . your stomach will bloat with gas which can't escape because your bowels haven't anything to do.'

She remained silent.

'I know . . . I've seen it before. Twelve times. But I've told you that.' He tossed a small piece of meat on to the floor in front of her, easily within her reach. He watched as Linda Handy looked at it, forced herself to remain still, but eventually could no longer resist the temptation to snatch it up and put it in her mouth. 'See . . . knew you were getting peckish.'

'Why are you doing this?' She chewed the meat slowly.

'It's fun . . . gives me a sense of power. You know I have told the police that when I contact them I will use the code word "Dance Master" because I am leading them a merry dance. It's fun . . . it's power. You like the meat? I'd like to give you some more, but I can't. It's not allowed.'

'Allowed? Who by?'

'The rules of the game says it's not allowed. But I don't think one little lump will matter . . . since you won't be getting another one. I just wanted to see for myself that the old hunger pangs are kicking in.'

'So you've seen . . . and they are.'

'Did you hear the owl in the night?' He glanced out of the window beside him, 'Old tawny owl, he's been living here for a while . . . keeps the mice down . . . to-wit . . . to-woo. Did you hear him?'

'Yes.'

'And not much else?'

'No.'

'You see, that's why you can scream all you like, because there is no one to hear you. But if you wake me up by screaming, I will pour ice-cold water over you: give you something else to contend with as well as hunger, a nice dose of pneumonia to meet your maker with.'

'The police will be looking for me.'

He put his knife and fork down. 'Oh, do me a favour, they might if they knew where to look. They can't search all the houses in York, not in the time they've got when other duties have to be performed . . . and anyway, you're not in York, are you? You're in the sticks, way out in the sticks.' He ate another mouthful. 'Lovely lunch this, all my own work. I like cooking . . . just survival cooking

like most bachelors, but at least I do it. Some guys live
off takeaways but not this guy.' He inclined a thumb to
his chest. 'This guy is independent ... independent in
thought and action. I look after myself, I cook for myself,
clean for myself, fend for myself.' He ate another mouthful
of his meal. 'You know, I contacted the police by leaving
a message with a newspaper out Liverpool way ...
wonderful thing the telephone, shielded my number, could
have been calling from anywhere. Next call I make will
be a newspaper in Scotland or maybe Wales or in the deep
south of England. Where is there in the south of England?
Name a town.'

'Brighton,' she said, remembering enjoyable childhood
holidays.

'Brighton will do nicely. We can play this game. When
I want to phone the boys in blue, do you know what I'll
do? Hey, that rhymes. Did you hear what I said?' He
smiled. 'I said, when I phone the boys in blue, this is what
I'll do. I like that. Anyway, what I'll do is tell you the
area of the country I want to phone and you can tell me
a town. So, if I say Wales you say ... well, what will you
say?'

'Swansea,' she replied, holding eye contact and smiling
as if she too was enjoying the game.

'OK ... and if I say Scotland?'

'Edinburgh.'

'OK. Well not OK. You see, I want small towns not
big cities. I want you to think of small towns, so let's try
again.' He finished the meal, tossed the knife and fork on
to the plate and pushed the plate away from him in what
Linda Handy thought to be an ill-mannered, rough gesture.
'There's some scraps left,' he said, 'but you can't have
them. They're going to my pigs ... the scraps. So, deep
south of England? Where?'

'I don't know ... I don't know the south.'

The man's smile vanished in an instant. He froze her with a piercing-eyed scowl. 'Think! How old are you?'

'Thirty-seven?'

'Lived in England all your life?'

'Yes . . . yes.'

'So think of a small town in the south of England. I'm getting angry . . . don't make me angry . . . angry . . . I get bad when people make me angry . . . bad, bad, bad.'

'Ramsgate!'

The man smiled. 'Alright, I'm not angry now. See, you have given me what I want . . . see how life is easier for you if you don't make me angry. Do you?'

'Yes, I do.' Still speaking softly, warmly, still holding eye contact.

'So, Wales . . . and don't say you don't know, and I want a name I can pronounce.'

'Carmarthen. How about Carmarthen?'

'Aye . . . I like it. And Scotland . . . small town in Scotland?'

'Falkirk, that's a small town.'

'Well, it's not a city, so I'll take your word for it, pet.' He paused and patted his stomach. 'Love food. Anyway, what I'll do is ask you for the name of a small town in a part of Britain and you give me a name, then I phone directory enquiries and ask them for the telephone number of the library in that town. See?'

'Yes.'

'Then I shield my number and phone the library and ask if there is a small local newspaper in the area, they'll give me the name and possibly the telephone number as well. If they can't give me the number, I'll phone directory enquiries again and get the number from them. Then I'll phone the paper . . . with a shielded number . . . explain who I am and ask them to phone the police in York. The guy in charge of the case is an old guy called Hennessey

. . . his picture was in the *Yorkshire Post*. So, message for DCI Hennessey, code word "Dance Master", and that will come from a small newspaper local to Ramsgate, and the next one, a small newspaper local to Carmarthen and the one after that a small newspaper local to Falkirk because you've said them . . . you say other names . . . you can think of them tonight when I'm at work.'

Again Linda Handy wondered what sort of farmer was this man, what sort of farm was she imprisoned upon that this man sleeps late, lunches heavily, leaves for work at about 6 p.m. and returns at midnight. She sensed though, that he was dangerous, very dangerous, unpredictable, and further sensed she had better not ask questions.

Somerled Yellich drove home. He was not displeased with his afternoon's work. A trawl of the missing persons files had whittled down the list of 'potential abductees' who might be linked to the bones in the plastic Whitelands bag. It had been a day spent in the confines of Micklegate Bar Police Station in the void, in the archives, alone at a desk, recording dusty files, each one a heart-rending tale of a family's anguish about the disappearance of a loved one. Visits would have to be done upon the morrow, hoping that the families might be able to provide something from which the DNA profile of the missing person might be extracted and matched with the DNA profile in the bones.

He turned into the Huntingdon estate and drew up along-side his home. As he did so, the door opened and Jeremy ran out to meet him, running at him with such force that he caused Yellich to step backwards upon impact.

'Been a good boy?'

'Yes, Daddy.' Jeremy walked beside Yellich into the house, where his wife stood in the kitchen, baking. She looked, to Yellich, to be exhausted and all she could manage was a bleary-eyed smile and a weak 'Hello.'

'Bad day?'

'He's been hyper since he came home from school . . . not misbehaving, just energetic.'

'I'll take him for a walk, give you a bit of space.'

'I'd appreciate it. Think I've got a result, as I think you would say, on the van.'

'Really?'

'Well, see what you think. Space first . . . woman needs space . . . woman craves space and calming noise from Radio Four . . . much calming noise.'

Yellich walked round the estate and out to the fields beyond, with his son holding on to his arm, identifying trees and naming plants. Jeremy Yellich, now aged twelve in real years, but several less in mental years, had brought much joy to his parents and a whole new unknown world had been opened for them. Jeremy's childhood, his innocence, had been prolonged because of his condition and he would never be the rebellious teenager dreaded by many parents. Because of him the Yellichs had met other parents of children with 'learning difficulties', children who used to be dismissed as 'mentally handicapped'. Friendships had been formed, real and lasting ones, and which Yellich knew would still be extant when Jeremy moved into the hostel. They walked for a blustery hour and returned home with reddened cheeks and noses and then Yellich sat with Jeremy as Jeremy pointed to each letter of the alphabet as he randomly dictated them. Later, by using an old clock, Jeremy turned the hands and showed a delighted and impressed Somerled Yellich that he had mastered 'hard' times like twenty-two minutes to two.

'So,' said Yellich, 'tell me about the result you might have got?'

'Well –' Sara Yellich sipped her tea – 'lady came to the door . . . not long before you came home . . . said a white van used to be parked outside a house in Broome

Drive. She didn't know the number but it was the house on the corner of Broome Drive and Broome Avenue, a detached house, and definitely Broome Drive. About five years ago.'

'Interesting.'

'The lady said she knew that because her sister lived in the house across the street and saw it often when she visited but she didn't know whether it belonged to the house or was a visitor's car.'

'I'll take a stroll round there now . . . seven p.m. . . . not late.' He finished his mug of tea, drinking from his favourite mug, which was cream with a bold red heart on the outside and a large black 'I' and 'Dad' on either side of the heart – it had been bought for him by Sara and Jeremy on a day trip they had made to Scarborough two summers previously.

'Wrap up –' Sara Yellich unentwined her arm from that of her husband – 'the wind's getting up.'

Yellich wrapped up – duffel coat and scarf – and strolled the few hundred yards from his home to Broome Drive. The visit transpired to be brief, the present owners of the house having moved in only two years earlier. They could tell Yellich little about the person from whom they had bought the house, believing her to be a single woman and further believing her not to be a car owner. If there was a van regularly seen outside the house, it must have been a visitor, they suggested.

'Must have been,' Yellich nodded. 'Where do you forward her mail?'

'Very little arrives now, but what did arrive, we handed it in at the estate agents through whom the house was sold, Giles, Chapple and Lane, George Hudson Street, York.'

'Thanks,' Yellich smiled, 'that helps. Points us in a direction.'

*   *   *

Later that same windy night Sandra Tupper was walking home. She was wearing a black coat and black boots on a dark night.

Ideal.

The man came up behind her wearing soft-soled shoes and brought the hammer down upon her head. She crumpled silently. The man carried her to the waste ground and hit her twice more. Then calmly, very calmly, walked away.

Five

in which a hermit-like lady makes a distressing identification and Yellich meets a ruined and remorseful young woman.

SATURDAY, 09.00 HOURS – 18.45 HOURS

The man walked into the room carrying his breakfast. 'Kippers,' he said, though the woman refused to look up at him. 'Boil-in-the-bag kippers, even I can cook them without going wrong. You like the smell?' He sat down at the table and began to eat. He turned to the woman. 'If you don't want me to pour cold water over you, you'd better answer, Linda Handy. Do you like the smell?'

'Yes, I like the smell.' She spoke through gritted teeth. The pain in her stomach was constant. Her body felt weaker.

'Good. I am glad you like the smell. I like the smell too. I like the taste even better. Would you like to taste some?'

'Yes, I would.' Again spoken through gritted teeth.

'Pity, eh?' The man forked oiled kipper into his mouth. 'I mean that you can't have a taste, not even a little bit. You realize you will probably never eat again?'

'The thought had crossed my mind.' She still refused to look at him.

'Did a good job with you, spiriting you away in broad daylight. I did it with the others but only when I got good at it. I did the first nine at night . . . the last three I did during the day, enjoyed the risk.' He dropped the fork on the plate. 'See, pet, the more risks you take, the more fun there is in getting away with it and nobody saw me . . . broad daylight . . . road . . . houses about and no one saw anything. Well, if they did, they're not telling.'

'What's that you sprayed in my eyes?'

'Pepper spray, Mace it's called. Can't get it in England, but I have a cousin in the States, he sends it to me, all the way from sunny Arry-zone . . . ah. Always works. Then a bang on the head and, well, you know the rest.' He stood and walked to an easy chair and sank in it.

Linda Handy felt his eyes upon her, as she had felt men's eyes upon her in her younger years, as if mentally peeling her clothing away layer by layer, but he hadn't tried anything. If he hadn't tried anything by then, she reasoned, he is unlikely to try anything at all. At least it appeared she was going to be spared that indignity.

'Didn't leave them much,' the man mused. 'No witnesses, just a rough tyre track in the grass verge, but not enough to bring them to me.'

'You want to be caught?' This time she glanced up at him, briefly so. She saw him shrug his shoulders.

'Perhaps I do,' he said.

Again she thought him insane.

'I bet you think I'm mad, don't you?'

She didn't reply.

'Don't you?'

'I think you're strange, you seem to want to be caught, I would have thought you'd want the opposite.'

'Well, I am mad.'

A chill shot through her.

'I am . . . seriously . . . I've been in the loony bin.' He smiled. 'See, I did it again, that rhymes. I've been in the loony bin, kept me for a while, then let me go but I do things, can't stop myself. I know it's wrong but I still do them.'

'You don't have to do bad things.'

'Oh, but I do, you see, that's just it, pet. I do have to do bad things, there are no voices in my head telling me what to do, nothing like that, like you read about, but there's just this urge to do bad things. I mean the only bad things I do is kill people, that's all.'

'That's all?' she gasped.

'Yes . . . I mean, I don't damage people's property, I'm an honest man, I don't steal, I don't assault people once they're mine. I never do anything like that.'

'You just kill people.' She kept her eyes downcast, looking at the floor. 'That's bad enough.'

'Yes, but that's all, and I do it slowly. I know it's wrong but I can't stop myself. I have plenty of time to stop myself, but I can't once the urge to kill gets me, so I want to be stopped . . . I want them to catch me and stop me.'

'You could hand yourself in.'

'I can't do that. That's not in the rules.'

'The rules?'

'Of the game . . . this game has rules, it's a game of catch. I run, they catch, but they've got to know who to catch, and I can't just walk into the police station . . . that's not playing the game. They've only got a few days to find me before your body starts eating itself. Right now you're living on your fat reserves.'

'You told me.'

'So I helped them.'

'You helped them?'

'Yes . . . last night, I murdered someone.'

Linda Handy felt as though she had been kicked in the stomach. 'You killed someone?'

'Yes . . . I did it for you, Linda, I hope you realize that, I hope you realize what I did for you.'

'For me . . . ?'

'Yes, you see I left her there, by now they will have discovered her body. I didn't take her away like the others, and I am going to make a phone call so they will know it's me, it'll help them catch me. If they catch me, they might save you. Are you cold, pet?'

'Yes . . . in the night it got cold.'

'I'll fetch a blanket for you. Then I'll go out, make that phone call. What's the name of a town in the south of England?'

'I thought of one for you in the night . . . Wimborne, I went there once, it's in Dorset, a pretty town, really small.'

'Wimborne . . . I haven't heard of it, so it must be small. I'll phone the local paper, tell them it's "Dance Master", it'll liven their lives up, liven them up no end.' He began to laugh, uncontrollably.

Hennessey turned his head away as the crime scene examiner lifted the camera. He didn't want to be blinded by the flash. He then walked out of the inflatable tent which had been erected over the body of the woman and joined Yellich. Small crowds of curious people stood in isolated groups beyond the blue and white police tape which had been erected round the edge of the waste ground on which the body had been found. He walked over to where Yellich stood. The two men held brief eye contact. 'It's your day off tomorrow, isn't it?' Hennessey asked.

'Yes, skipper.'

'I am going to have to ask that you come in.'

Yellich nodded. 'I understand . . . I'll be able to square it with Sara.'

'Good man.' Rain began to fall and both men turned their coat collars up. 'Who found her?'

'Paper lad, doing his round. Dr Mann attended with myself and two uniformed officers, confirmed life extinct, erected the tent, called yourself and the pathologist.'

'Any ID?'

'Sandra Tupper . . . her handbag was by the body, has her bus pass, photograph on the bus pass appears to be her but as you see, she is face down, didn't want to move the body until Dr D'Acre has examined her. Couldn't move the body, I mean, not didn't want to, but the indication is that it is Sandra Tupper. Long black hair . . .'

'It's interesting the handbag wasn't stolen.'

'Yes, I thought that too, boss, not rifled either. Her purse has about twenty pounds in it plus credit cards, again in the name of Sandra Tupper. She lives . . . lived locally, next of kin have to be informed. This on top of "Dance Master" and the bag of bones.'

'It's going to stretch us alright . . . ah.' Hennessey smiled as he watched a red and white Riley RMA *circa* 1947 drive slowly towards the scene and stop at the kerb close to where the blue and white police tape hung limply, having been suspended between a lamppost and a telegraph pole. He continued to watch as Dr D'Acre opened the near hingeing driver's door and swivelled on her bottom, keeping her knees and ankles together and left the car 'both out together' in a practised, ladylike manner. She declined the offer of a young constable to carry her black Gladstone bag and carried it as she walked towards the tent. She was slender, short haired, late 40s, and her walk, her gait, betrayed a well-toned body beneath the green coverall she wore.

'Good morning, Chief Inspector, Sergeant.' Dr D'Acre smiled at the two officers.

'Morning, ma'am,' he replied for both himself and Yellich.

'What have we?'

'Body of a young adult female, ma'am. Dr Mann, the police surgeon, pronounced life extinct at . . .' Hennessey glanced at Yellich.

'Eight fifteen this morning, ma'am.'

'I see.' Dr D'Acre stepped forward and pulled aside the flap of the tent doorway. 'Yes . . . I see. I'll wait until your boys have finished taking their snaps, not a great deal of room in those tents.'

'Indeed, ma'am.'

'Anything we know about the victim?'

'We believe we know her identity. Unsure of the motive for murder.'

'If, indeed, it is murder.' Dr D'Acre spoke softly and raised an eyebrow. 'Only I can tell you that, Detective Chief Inspector. Let's not rush our fences.'

'Of course.' Hennessey smiled and attempted eye contact but Dr D'Acre wouldn't permit it, turning her head away from his gaze.

'Massive amount of dried blood in the hair at the back of the head,' Yellich offered. 'Be surprised if it was an accident.'

'That sounds suspicious, that I concede . . . but it's still my department, not yours.'

'Yes, ma'am . . . I wasn't . . .'

'No matter.' D'Acre smiled. 'I'm sure you are right.'

The two crime scene examiners emerged from the tent. 'All finished in there, sir . . . black and white and colour from every angle.'

'Thanks,' Hennessey nodded.

'Well . . . we'll see if you are right.' Dr D'Acre stepped forward and entered the tent. Hennessey followed. Yellich remained outside.

In the tent, Dr D'Acre knelt by the body and opened her Gladstone bag. She took out a thermometer. 'I know that you'll want time of death.'

'It might be useful.' Hennessey remained standing, and kept a respectful distance from Dr D'Acre and the corpse.

'Strictly speaking, we are not supposed to give it . . . cause of death, determination of, is our area of expertise and responsibility, what the Home Office pays us for, but, I'll be of what help I can. I'll take a rectal recording and then a ground temperature recording and work up the results later.' Dr D'Acre lifted and pulled the lower garments of the deceased and inserted the rectal thermometer into the rectum of the young woman and observed the mercury. 'Quite cold . . . barely above freezing, killed last night possibly . . . two degrees Celsius.' She removed the thermometer and re-covered the deceased's buttocks with her skirt and coat. The dead must have their dignity, being the clear attitude Hennessey believed Dr D'Acre to have. 'The ground temperature is about the same, but the top coat and shoes and the smart skirt should tell you that she had probably been out for the night and that she was not found until this a.m. ought to pinpoint her time of death.'

'Killed whilst returning home?'

'Yes. Frankly, Chief Inspector, logical deduction is often a far more accurate method of determining the time of death than anything I can tell you. So let's see what I can tell you.' She examined the head of the deceased. 'Well, Sergeant Yellich was certainly right about the blood in her hair and I suspect that he will be correct that she was murdered . . . a brutal attack from behind with a blunt object.'

'As you say.'

Dr D'Acre continued her examination. 'The clothing is intact. I was the first to disturb her clothing when I took the rectal temperature, so I doubt if we will find any indication of sexual assault, which might be worrying for you, Chief Inspector . . . and here I encroach on your department.'

'Oh, encroach all you like, ma'am, but why worrying?'

'Well, the handbag was left at the scene . . . no indication of a sexual assault. She was not discovered until this morning, otherwise I would have been called out earlier, so the reason she was not robbed or sexually assaulted was not because her attacker was disturbed and had to flee. So the motive, if there is one, is either very personal or non-existent . . . the random attack, she was in the wrong place at the wrong time. If it's the latter, then the person might strike again . . . they got a taste for it . . . just what you don't need when you have the "Bag of Bones" investigation on your plate.'

'Yes, that has occurred to us.'

'Well, there are no other apparent injuries, just the blunt trauma to the skull. If you have finished, I will remove her to the York City Hospital. ID before the PM, I presume?'

'Yes, I think so.' Hennessey spoke softly. 'Her face isn't damaged . . . bad news for someone . . . I know what they are going to go through.'

Uncharacteristically, Dr D'Acre looked up at Hennessey and held eye contact and said, 'Yes.'

Hennessey left Yellich to supervise the conveying of the body in a body bag on a stretcher to the waiting black, windowless van for onward conveyance to the hospital, in which, hardened by their job, the driver and his mate sat smoking cigarettes and reading tabloid newspapers. He also asked Yellich to arrange a sweep of the waste ground once the body had been removed. He undertook to visit the home of Sandra Tupper, which stood a few hundred yards from where her body was found.

The home address of Sandra Tupper was typical Holgate, YO26, a terraced house, the front door of which abutted the pavement. The door paint was peeling and faded, the home being south-facing. Hennessey pressed the doorbell and hearing no noise from within, knocked on the door. There was still no response. Hennessey knocked again and this time a rasping female voice said, 'Who is it?'

'Police,' Hennessey raised his voice sufficiently to ensure it carried into the house. He was aware of people in closely packed terraced houses standing in their doorways watching him. This was clearly an 'event' in the street and will be the talk of the pub that lunchtime and evening, and doubtless, he thought, for many days to come. A particularly large woman walked confidently up to him in a manner which clearly suggested she was the matriarch of the street.

'So, it's Sandra?'

'I'm sorry?' Hennessey turned to her, holding his ground. He sensed the woman was used to folk backing away from her.

'The lass that was found on the waste ground . . . it was Sandra Tupper? You're a cop, you walked from the waste ground, I followed you . . . came straight to this house, don't need to be a brain surgeon to put two and two together.'

'Wait a minute,' the voice came from inside the house.

'Can't tell you.' Hennessey turned away from the large woman.

'Well, you'll be surprised what you find in there, Sandra was always so well turned out, so smartly dressed, she did well to be like that.'

'And you are?'

'Just a neighbour. Just wait till you see her mum, Pearl Tupper by name.'

'Won't you give me your name?'

'Why?'

'You seem to know Sandra.'

'So it is her?' The woman smiled a very self-satisfied smile.

'Still can't say.' Hennessey had to concede that point to the woman. She had trapped him, tripped him up, cleverly so. He thought she had probably left school with no qualifications to stack shelves at the nearest supermarket, but was clearly possessed of a brain which, had she been given different messages about herself when growing up, and had she chosen to use it, could have catapulted herself well out of these streets of mean, dark houses.

'Well, I'll leave you at it.' The big woman turned on her heels and walked towards a small group of women who had gathered at the door of one of the residents and said in a voice loud enough for Hennessey to hear, 'It's Sandra Tupper alright, he's as good as told me,' and brought a gasp from the group, which Hennessey, using the reflection in the window at the side of the door, saw fragment, with the women walking rapidly in several directions, doubtless to spread the news of the end of Sandra Tupper of Holgate.

The door was flung open. Hennessey gasped, for the occupant of the house was, he thought, hag-like.

'Aye?' She glared at Hennessey with cold, green eyes. She was short, about five feet tall, he guessed, with whiskers surrounding a thin-lipped mouth. It was difficult for him to age her.

'Mrs Tupper?'

'Aye.' Her stale breath smelled of alcohol and tobacco.

'I may have some bad news for you.'

'Our Sandra, what's she gone and done now?'

Although he didn't relish the prospect of doing so, Hennessey said, 'I think we had better talk inside.'

Inside the back-to-back terraced house was just as Hennessey had feared: sticky carpets which tugged at the soles of his shoes as he walked on them, stuffy air which comes of not opening any windows for months at a time, a glance in the kitchen revealed piles of unwashed plates and cups, and an ashtray balanced precariously on the arm of an easy chair was long overdue for emptying.

'So, what's wrong?' Mrs Tupper had an aggressive attitude, to Hennessey's mind.

'You have a daughter . . . Sandra?'

'I just said I did . . . there's just me and her in the house, she's a bit, . . . well, like I'm not good enough for her . . . her so clean all the time. So, what's wrong?'

'I'm afraid she may have been murdered, Mrs Tupper.'

The woman caught her breath. 'What's she want to go and have herself killed for?'

'I hardly think it was a question of choice, Mrs Tupper –' Hennessey found himself speaking in an angry manner – 'not on her part anyway.'

'But . . . she's dead . . . you're telling me she's dead?'

'We think it's her. We'd like to ask you to identify the body, tell us it is Sandra.'

'Where?'

'At the mortuary department at York City Hospital.'

'Can't you bring it here?'

'It?'

'The body . . . can't you bring it here?'

'Mrs Tupper, this is likely, all but certainly your

daughter we are talking about. "It" is hardly the word I would choose under these circumstances.'

'Aye . . . but I haven't been out of the house in twenty years. Right from when she was a little lassie, Sandra's done all the shopping for us . . . everything . . . I've never been out, not since the day my man left us.'

'Well, I'm afraid I will have to insist . . . we'll go in a car.'

'A car?'

'Yes, so you'll only have to walk from the door across the pavement to a car . . . take you there and bring you back.'

'And bring me back?'

'Yes.'

'I don't have a coat . . . grew out of my last one . . . never go out so don't need one.'

'Well it's not raining at the moment, if you've got a sweater or something? But really you'll be in the car in no time and the car will drop us right at the hospital door.'

'Alright.'

'When did you last see your daughter?'

'Yesterday evening, she was going out to a nightclub, all dressed up like she was the Queen of the May.'

'The Queen of the May,' Hennessey repeated. The archaic expression appealed to him: he hadn't heard it for many years and images of maypole dancing and other pagan rituals to welcome the spring flooded into his mind. 'What time did you expect her home?'

'When she went out she stayed out late, came home after midnight, she could still get up for her work in the morning. She works on Saturdays in a supermarket . . . a manageress. Sometimes she stays out all night, never brings her boyfriends home though . . . always stays at their house. I don't like her doing that, but she's a woman grown, it's her body.'

'Is it her practice to walk home at night?'

'I don't know, I never go out, I don't know what her practice is. I've heard cars stop outside and Sandra get out. If it's a man friend or a taxi . . . that I couldn't ever say.'

'I see, so you wouldn't know who her friends are?'

'No, she never brings them home, she stopped bringing her friends home when she was a little lassie. I'm not good enough for her . . . happy to stay here, though . . . So she's got herself killed.'

'Do you mind if I have a look in her room?'

'Why?'

'Because there might be something in her room which could tell us who she was with last night.'

'Room at the back.' Mrs Tupper reached for a packet of cigarettes, clawed it open and roughly extracted a cigarette which she lit with an inexpensive lighter. 'Dead . . .' she said to herself, but clearly heard by Hennessey. 'Dead . . . who's going to do the shopping now?'

Hennessey climbed the narrow stairway, cold, dark, dank, yet opening the door to the back room was like opening the door to a ray of sunshine, for here, like an oasis, was the opposite of that which surrounded it. For Sandra Tupper's bedroom was neat, clean, tidy . . . a reaction to her mother's lifestyle, a reaction against it. Hennessey pondered the hard work that must have gone into keeping a room in this pleasant state within a house like Mrs Tupper's. Hennessey opened drawers: he turned up an address book with disappointingly few entries. He put it back in the drawer. Sandra Tupper, he found, also kept a journal which had been written up to the previous Thursday, but gave no indication as to whom she had intended to visit the nightclub with the following evening. This too he replaced. Both books could be consulted again if need be. The photograph of a young woman leaning against a red sports car told Hennessey that the strange and dread Mrs Tupper below, at that moment doubtless pulling heavily on a cigarette, would shortly leave her house for the first time in twenty years and, at the hospital, make a positive identification, and be returned home to wonder who would now be doing the shopping.

Downstairs once more, Hennessey went outside and plunged his hand into his coat pocket and extracted his mobile phone. He phoned Micklegate Bar Police Station and requested a car be sent to collect him and Mrs Tupper to take them to York District Hospital and to return Mrs Tupper later. The crowd of neighbours had recongregated – in fact, Hennessey thought, it had grown slightly, curious about the tragedy, curious too, perhaps, to see the hermit-like, reclusive Mrs Tupper, some for the first time in twenty years, some for the first time at all.

'It won't,' Hennessey said as they waited for the car to arrive, 'be like what you might have seen on television. She won't be pulled out of a bank of drawers and a blanket pulled back . . . it's more sensitive than that these days. You'll look at her through a pane of glass. She'll be lying on a trolley, well tucked up with blankets, as though she's floating in space. All you'll see is her face. She'll look quite at peace.'

Half an hour later, Mrs Tupper said, 'Aye, that's our Sandra. That's my little lassie . . . but who'll do the shopping now? I mean, who'll do it? Who?'

'Yes, Miss Magg. Strange lady, very quiet, very secretive. I recall that sale, it went through very quickly . . . no chain, you see. She wasn't moving into another house, just wanted cash in the bank.' Norman South, by the nameplate on his desk, was a man in his forties, Yellich guessed; short, a little overweight, heavy black-framed spectacles which seemed to belong to a different era and which, thought Yellich, did not particularly suit him; a lighter, metal-framed pair would sit better on his face. He spoke with a strong Yorkshire accent.

'We'd really like to trace her.'

'I don't think it will be easy.' Norman South leaned forward in his chair, elbows on his desk top. Behind him were photographs of houses being marketed on behalf of their owners by Giles, Chapple and Lane, estate agents, George Hudson Street, York. 'She just disappeared.'

'Disappeared?'

'As good as . . . nothing sinister, nothing for you chaps to worry about . . . nothing criminal. It's as though Miss Magg wanted to sever all ties with York and start fresh somewhere else. She was a young woman, still in her twenties, there was time yet for her to start afresh somewhere.'

'Did she give any reason why she would want to do that, Mr South?'

'Not to us, and frankly that's not the sort of thing an estate agent would be privy to anyway. The present owners used to bring Miss Magg's mail into us . . . it was all junk really . . . and eventually we advised them just to chuck it unless it was obviously not junk, but they never brought anything to us after that, so I presume that Miss Magg had been thorough in notifying her friends, family and acquaintances of her new address.'

'What did you do with the mail that was brought to you?'

'Sent it on to the solicitor she engaged to act for her in the house sale.'

'Who was?'

'And still is . . . Simpson and Mason. She was represented by a Mr Pugh of that firm.'

'Pugh.' Yellich committed the name to memory. 'That
firm is on Swinegate, is it not?'

'Yes . . , surprised you know it, they don't do crime
work at all, all conveyancing and civil litigation.'

'I must have just seen the sign –' Yellich smiled –
'when walking in the city centre.'

'Must have.'

'Do you know what Miss Magg did for a living?'

'School teacher. That's strange as well . . . sold her house
during term time, left York in the middle of term. Very
strange for a teacher. I think their contracts stipulate that
they must not leave their posts during full term . . . even
leaving at half term is frowned on.'

'I can check. My wife used to be a teacher. I can ask
her, but as you say, it's very strange . . . and leaving
York like she did.'

'Oh dear.' Norman South sat back in his chair. 'You
don't think . . . ?'

'That she committed a crime and left in shame?' Yellich,
reading South's mind, completed the sentence for him.
'Well, it's a possibility. I can very easily check. If it is
the case, we'll be able to obtain her present address without
having to wait until Monday when Simpson and Mason
will be open for business, possibly anyway.'

'Possibly? They will be open, it's not a bank holiday
on Monday.'

'No, I meant we might possibly obtain Miss Magg's
present address before Monday.'

'I see, sorry.'

'Did you deal with her, you personally?'

'Yes. What brief contact we had with the young lady
was with myself. But as you'll probably know yourself
in such circumstances, the greater contact is with the

solicitor, rather than the estate agent.'

'Yes . . . yes.'

'But I visited the property, took measurements for the schedule . . . told her to tidy the house up and also the garden. The garden was small, but jungle-like. She had a new-build house in Huntingdon.'

'Yes, I know. I live on the same estate.'

'Really?'

'Yes. What was her manner when you met her?'

'Well, come to think of it, she seemed preoccupied and it did cross my mind that she, a teacher, was at home during the school day . . . She was unkempt, slovenly dressed, hair everywhere, ashtrays full of fag ash . . . empty gin bottle on the TV . . . not the sort of house you would expect a maths teacher to keep.'

'How did you know she taught maths?'

'Maths text books on a small desk in the corner of the room.' South smiled. 'In my job you get to read folks' homes, as I imagine the police also do?'

'Yes, we are trained to read streets and the inside of folks' houses. There is much you can glean in a glance and first impressions are usually accurate. A *Guardian* lying about will probably mean you have got a civil liberties bloke on your hands, a *Daily Telegraph* and he'll be a law and order guy . . . fastidiously kept households will mean an oppressive head of the house or at least an illiberal person. A clean, but untidy house with stuff lying about will be the home of a more liberal-minded person. But we also learn not to jump to conclusions, just gain an impression, that's the purpose of reading rooms.' Yellich paused. 'And Miss Magg's house was?'

'"Shambolic" would be the work I'd use to describe it.'

'Do you recall her first name?'

'Holly.' Norman South smiled. 'Holly Magg . . . not only does it have a ring to it, but it's the name my wife and I chose for our firstborn and only daughter . . . she was born within the twelve days . . . and we wanted a name to suit the season and time of year. Holly was perfect, we toyed with Ivy but thought it too nineteenth century. Our other children were boys . . . two boys and a girl . . . girl and two boys to put them in the right order.'

'Holly Magg.' Yellich took out his notepad and wrote the name on it. 'So that was how long ago?'

'About five years. It's one that sticks in my mind for some reason. Some you remember, some you forget . . . you just do.'

'Yes . . . yes and she was in her twenties then?'

'Late twenties, I'd say. Selling up quite early. Couldn't have been in the house very long, not a lot of equity, I would have thought. Be in her early to mid thirties now.'

'Yes . . . yes.'

'One of the easy ones.' Dr D'Acre rested her hands on the stainless-steel dissecting table, one of the four in the pathology laboratory of York District Hospital. 'Her skull is like a piece of crazy paving. No other injuries at all. Somebody came up behind her and whacked her over the head with what might be a ball-pein hammer.'

'One rounded head?'

'Yes, also called balled hammers. The skull fracturing is consistent with that. The crazy paving seems to emanate from distinct points, four in all . . . *whack*, *whack*, *whack* and *whack*.'

'He or she was making sure, seems like.'

'Yes, very sure. Just one might have been fatal, two would have been, but four . . . making sure alright. She had eaten, sensible girl. Confess I am worried about my own daughters, they are beginning to pick at their food rather than eat it. Not a problem yet, but I am keeping my eye on it.'

'I can understand the worry.'

'But the mother or parents of young Miss Tupper here . . .'

'Mother.'

'Yes, sorry, you said. The mother of Miss Tupper hadn't that worry. She ate sensibly, looks like a chicken kebab . . . a night at the dancing, Friday night out, a kebab . . . walking home.'

'Nearly made it too, just another few hundred yards.'

Louise D'Acre turned and once again allowed brief and very uncharacteristic eye contact with Hennessey. 'Yes,' she said, 'it just goes to show, even in your own street you're not safe. Do you know how old she was? Twenties definitely.'

'Twenty-three.'

'Oh . . . all suspicious deaths have their poignancy, but the younger the person, the more the poignancy.'

'Indeed,' said Hennessey, for the want of something to say, but the death of a woman when aged 23 had a resonance with him.

'You found me quite easily.' Holly Magg sat on a large cushion in the corner of her room.

'Phoned the probation service. They have a duty worker on Saturdays.'

'Oh.'

'In case a court sits . . . special sittings . . . has been known.'

'Even though I am no longer on probation?' She had a mop of straggly black hair, wore a grey smock over faded blue jeans, and had 'flip-flop' sandals on her feet.

121

The room was spartan, cold in temperature, cold in atmosphere, cold in 'feel'. Yellich wondered at her feet, naked save for little plastic sandals that were attached to her feet with a single loop for the big toe.

'Well, all they could give me was your last known address. I called on the off chance.'

'So, I'm not in trouble?'

'Don't know . . . are you?'

She inclined her head and smiled at Yellich as if to say 'clever'.

'Well, I have enough regret for one lifetime, I don't need any more, so I keep out of folks' way. I'd leave York if I could.'

'You can't?'

'No money, and my family is here, but occasionally I go into town and am terrified of meeting my old pupils or my old colleagues. I was on my way, maths teacher at a comprehensive school, mortgage on a house . . . I loved that house, it was small . . . on the Huntingdon estate, if you know it?'

'Yes –' Yellich spoke softly – 'a little.'

'Well, I was so proud, I grew up in council land . . . you see my father was a bus driver, my mother wasn't anything . . . I was their life. They were delighted when I made it to university and got a good degree and got the teaching post and I was so proud when I got my own home, no more paying rent for this one . . . now look at me, a one-bedroom flat in Tang Hall, back in council land, back paying rent. So, what can I do for the boys in blue, since I am not under suspicion?'

'Well.' Yellich adjusted his position in the upright chair in which he had been invited to sit. 'This is about the time that you lived in Huntingdon.'

'Oh, yes, the happy days.'

'We are led to believe that a white van was often parked

outside your house, and that you knew the driver of said vehicle.'

Holly Magg smiled and lifted her head briefly. 'He was my downfall.'

'So you do know him?'

'Knew . . . knew . . . knew. I knew of him, don't anymore, he ruined my life.'

'What happened?' Yellich glanced out of the window by which he sat and viewed the uniformity of the uniformly drab Tang Hall Estate, low-rise council development with small gardens for each block of flats, narrow roads and very few facilities. A place, like Cambridge House, where a person, when homeless, is 'put'.

'Never knew his name.' Holly Magg shook her head at her own folly. 'Shared my bed . . . never knew his name. Well, he told me a name, I knew him as Donald Carpenter . . . nice name . . . sort of solid.'

'But it wasn't his real name?'

'No, never knew his real name . . . he was . . . I don't know . . . he was, well dangerous, probably in a violent way, though I never saw any violence from him but he could make me do things I didn't want to do. I knew they were wrong, but I did them anyway.'

'Because he wanted you to?'

'Yes. I wanted to please him. I am hardly catwalk material and he was the first man to show any interest in me, so I wanted to please him . . . women do . . . they want to please the man in their life, and he was the only man I ever had in mine, of course I'd want to please him. We met in a pub and he looked at me with such warmth and approval in his eyes, I just melted . . . melted enough to tell him the layout of the school I worked in . . . melted enough to let him store some boxes at my house without checking what was in them.'

'What was in them?'

'Computers from the school's IT suite.'

'Oh.'

'Yes . . . oh . . . The police knew it had to be an inside job, a master key was used. All the staff have a master key which opens the internal doors. It's a health and safety thing really: in case there is a fire and a door is locked, the nearest member of staff will have a key which will unlock it. He must have got hold of my master key, had a copy made. So when it was seen that the door of the IT suite hadn't been forced, but unlocked, the police assumed a member of staff was involved, even though the school had actually been broken into . . . a window was forced.'

'But once in the school, the thief had free reign?'

'Thieves, there were two of them. The police were able to tell that, but yes, once inside the school, the thieves could go anywhere, because they had a master key . . . so, inside job. The police called on the houses of each member of staff from the headmaster down. Called on me and found the missing computers, complete with invisible ink, or whatever it is, infra-red marker which proved they were from the school. So I was done for conspiracy to steal and receiving stolen goods. I was lucky, really.'

'Lucky! You sound to have been used and deserted.'

'Yes. I was . . . had been . . . but it could have gone to a much higher court. In the event, it was dealt with by the magistrates with limited sentencing powers, not often wisely used, but still limited. I pleaded not guilty and hired an expensive lawyer. The trial was a mess, well, I was a mess, in floods of tears throughout. Anyway, their Worships found in my favour after retiring to deliberate . . . for conspiracy, that is. So I was found not guilty to that, but they said they couldn't get round the fact that wittingly, or unwittingly, I had allowed stolen goods to be stored in my house. The head beak said it was incumbent upon me to check what it was I was allowing into my house.'

'Which is true.'

'Yes . . . I know that now, but the way that man could influence me . . .'

'Is not a defence.'

'I know that now as well, knew it at the time really.' She glanced to one side as if wishing herself back in an earlier, happier phase. 'Anyway, they gave me three years' probation. They said that that was lenient but they took into account my genuine remorse and the fact that I had ruined my life. I was a professional woman, I had a career with an inflation-proof pension at the end of it all. I could realistically have hoped to retire as a head of department . . . maybe even a headship . . . but after just three years of teaching, I was where I am now, on the dole, rented flat, no hope of ever working again. The beak was right, that's the penalty I paid. I ran out of food yesterday, I don't get my dole until Tuesday, that's four days without food. I've been here before, I'll get through.'

'So what happened to Donald Carpenter?'

'Vanished. Never saw him again. Doubt if that was his name.'

'Well, we want to have a chat with him. I'm sure you'd want to help us find him, be a bit of some settling for you.'

'Yes . . . anything I can tell you.'

'Well that's the nail hit well on the head,' Yellich smiled. He liked Holly Magg. 'Anything you can tell us.'

Hennessey returned to Micklegate Bar Police Station. There was a note in his pigeonhole which caused his heart to thump as he read it. The Editor of the *Wimborne*

Clarion wished to speak to him urgently in respect of 'Dance Master'. The call was timed earlier that afternoon, about the time Hennessey realized he had been in the pathology laboratory of York District Hospital, attending the post-mortem of Sandra Tupper for the police. Ignoring the other papers in his pigeonhole which he saw were clearly circulars, he clutched the telephone message and walked briskly to his office, where he snatched up the phone as he sat down at his desk. He jabbed '9' for an outside line. When the line clicked and he heard the soft purring of the outside-line-acquired tone, he rang the number given on the telephone message and asked to speak to the Editor.

'He's in a meeting, sorry.' The voice was female, soft, southern vowel sounds. 'He's not to be disturbed. Sorry.'

'He'll be disturbed for this.' Hennessey spoke calmly, but allowed a note of authority to edge into his voice. 'Tell him it's the police at York in respect of the telephone call he made to us earlier today. It is a matter of the utmost urgency that I speak to him.'

'Very good, sir.'

The line clicked and fell silent, giving Hennessey time to wriggle and shrug out of his raincoat as he felt the heat of the building become oppressive. Doesn't do, he thought, walking out of cold, drizzly conditions into a building where the heat, in his opinion, was always turned up so high that it couldn't possibly be healthy. He hung his coat on the stand and put his hat over it and sat at his desk as he heard a man's voice saying, 'Hello . . . anybody there? Sylvester at the *Clarion*.'

'Yes . . . sorry, Mr Sylvester, I was just getting out of my topcoat, it's far too warm in here, just got in, you see, and picked up your message. DCI Hennessey speaking.'

'Bad weather up there?'

'A little rain, need the coat for the cold in the main.'

'Ah . . . yes, mild and sunny down here.'

'Where is Wimborne? I'm sorry, I have never heard of it.'

'Dorset. If you have a map, find Bournemouth on the south coast, then look north.'

'Thanks. You received a phone call from somebody today calling himself "Dance Master"?'

'I did, didn't know what to make of it. I thought it was a crank call, but the man was very insistent. He said I should phone your good self, sir. He specifically mentioned you by name, Mr Hennessey, an easy name to remember, a fine Brandy by that name. Very fine indeed.'

'Spelled differently,' Hennessey said. 'I have an extra "e" but my name has been remembered by that means before now. So, the message?'

'Yes, a male, very strong north of England accent, really strong. Yes . . . he said the girl is getting hungry.'

'Yes . . . I know what that means. Anything else?'

'Indeed, there was, he said he was putting pressure on you. He said he did one last night . . .'

'Did one?'

'That's what he said. He said he "did the lassie well", he said he hit her four times on the head.'

Hennessey's scalp crawled.

'He said you'll find the hammer in the yellow privet near to where the body was.'

'The yellow privet?'

'Yes, he was insistent about that, repeated it three times and made me read it back to him. He said he wore gloves, so don't spend your time looking for prints.'

'OK.'

'Then he said I had to tell you that he was "Dance Master". He was very insistent upon that as well.'

127

'Yes, this gives this some credibility, it gives it complete credibility in fact. I would be obliged if you didn't mention this to anyone.'

'I mentioned it to my staff, we didn't know what to make of it.'

'Very well, I can understand that, but please ask them to keep it to themselves. It's a code word our man has decided upon. If it leaks, there'll be copycats.'

'Understood . . . leave it with me.'

'Appreciated. Now, what can you tell me about his voice, his manner . . . any background noise?'

'Haven't finished the message yet.'

'There's more?'

'Oh, yes, he said he'll be doing another one.'

'Oh, no . . .'

'Oh, yes.'

'Did he say when?'

'Soon.' Sylvester paused. 'He just said "soon". Then he said something which sent a chill down my flesh, made me think it might not be a crank call. He said, "I want them to stop us. I really want them to stop us. I don't like what I'm doing, but I can't stop us 'missen'." Curious, he speaks about two or three persons in "us" then the singular in "I", then the word "missen".'

'One person.' Hennessey changed the phone from his left to his right ear. 'In Yorkshire, folk talk about "us" when they mean "me".'

'How interesting.'

'It is really, if you are interested in regional dialects . . . broad Yorkshire is one of the oldest forms of spoken English, so I was told when I came here.'

'Yes, you don't sound like a northerner.'

'London by birth. I have been here for thirty years now, but when a Yorkshireman says, "I can't stop us," he can mean, "I can't stop myself."'

'I see, how interesting. I know about "thee" and "thou" and "thine" and "thy" as well, but not the use of "us" in the singular.'

'Yes, and the word you mentioned . . . ?'

'Sounded like "missen" with the emphasis on the second syllable.'

'Yes . . . missen . . . Yorkshire for "myself". He was saying, "I want to stop myself, I don't like what I am doing but I can't stop myself, by myself." But this must not be published, Mr Sylvester, not until he is apprehended and preferably until he has been convicted.'

'Understood and agreed.'

'Thank you.'

'Well, that was the sum of the message, Mr Hennessey. Quite sufficient for one such message and he didn't say why he called our small weekly newspaper because of an issue obtaining to York.'

'To avoid being traced.'

'Oh, he was traced.'

'What!'

'Oh, yes. Had he called a major national, they wouldn't have been able to trace the call from their busy switchboards, but we are a small and quiet office where the clock can be heard ticking upon ye wall, with a small and quiet switchboard. When I realized the call was probably not a crank, I scribbled a note to our junior to take to Vanessa on the switchboard, asking her not to answer any other call that might come in and then trace this one. She did as she was bid and when the call was terminated, she dialled 1471.'

'And?'

'The call came from York 621368 at ten forty hours.'

Hennessey scribbled the number on his pad. This, he said to himself, this was indeed gold dust.

'It was from a railway station.'

'You heard train announcements?'

'A platform alteration. "The Newcastle train will not depart from platform . . ." Can't remember the time nor the platform.'

'That could be York Station . . . direct line to Newcastle.'

'Sort of hubbub of noise in the background, not a whistle-stop on a country branch line. Ah . . . those were the days, when rail travel had a certain romance.'

'Well, thank you, Mr Sylvester, thank you indeed. This is possibly quite a breakthrough. Quite a breakthrough indeed.' Hennessey replaced the phone, snatched it up again, pressed nine for an outside line and phoned British Telecom. 'Police at Micklegate Bar,' he said after he was connected, 'we need to identify the location of a telephone number, possibly a call box.'

'I'll have to phone you back, sir, even if it is a public call box, someone might want to obtain the location of the number for nefarious reasons.' The operator was female, serious minded, sounded middle-aged.

'Very well . . . ask for me, DCI Hennessey.' He gave the telephone number of Micklegate Bar Police Station, then he hung up gently. It was frustrating but he felt he had to concede that the operator was right – have to be cautious, and procedures have to be followed. He sat and waited. He waited for thirty seconds and then his phone warbled. He picked it up. 'Hennessey.'

'Switchboard, sir. BT for you.'

'Thanks,' he said and heard the line click.

'Mrs Scales, BT.'

'Yes, Mrs Scales?'

'The number you gave is indeed a public payphone situated at York railway station, specifically it is in the foyer.'

'Thank you,' Hennessey scribbled the location of the

phone box on his notepad. 'Thank you again.' Once again he put the phone down and picked it up. On this occasion, he jabbed a four-figure internal number.

'Press Officer.'

'Hello, Hennessey speaking.'

'Yes, sir.' Like Mrs Scales of British Telecom, the press officer sounded to Hennessey to be a serious-minded middle-aged person, a male though, an officer taken from frontline duties, and as he listened to the voice, Commander Sharkey's warnings and entreaties echoed once more in Hennessey's mind.

'I'd like a press release organized.'

'Yes, sir.'

'Can you get the evening paper?'

'Final edition, yes, sir.'

'And the early-evening television and radio news?'

'Yes . . . plenty of time.'

'Good. The murder of Sandra Tupper in Holgate last night has been positively linked to the "Bag of Bones" murders.'

'Yes, sir, got that . . . good news for you, I would say.'

'How so?'

'Well, it means you haven't got two major inquiries after all.'

'Yes, that's some compensation, but we are not out of the woods, as you'll hear.' Hennessey paused. 'Then go on to say in words of your own choosing that the killer, using an agreed code word, has warned that he will kill again. People should avoid being out of doors late at night. This especially applies to young women.'

'Very good, sir, got that. I'll write it up in the form of a release. Shall I let you see it for your final approval?'

'No, I have faith and confidence in you.'

'Thank you, sir.'

131

Again Hennessey replaced the phone, but now he left it on the rest while he pondered his next move. He thought he could really use DS Yellich's presence but, being alone, he had to be in one place or the other: the recovery of the murder weapon or the British Transport Police to view their CCTV footage, in the hope that they were scanning the phone box at the time 'Dance Master' made the phone call to the *Wimborne Clarion*. One in the hand, he thought, was worth two in the bush. He leaned forward and picked up the phone, and again jabbed an internal number.

'Duty Officer.'

'DCI Hennessey. I'd like a van and six constables and a sergeant ready to leave for Holgate a.s.a.p.'

'Very good, sir . . . for you?'

'Yes.'

'Five minutes in the car park.'

'Excellent.'

Six minutes later, Hennessey and a sergeant and six constables were driven in a minibus the short distance between Micklegate Bar Police Station and the scene of the murder of Sandra Tupper in Holgate. The driver halted at the kerb at the edge of the waste ground where Sandra Tupper's battered body had been found, the blue and white police tape hanging forlornly from lampposts surrounding the murder scene. Hennessey glanced about him. On the other side of the road, at the far side of the waste ground, was a household whose front garden was bounded by a line of yellow privet, still clearly discernible in the fading light.

'Right, ladies and gentlemen.' Hennessey turned and addressed the sergeant and constables, two of whom were women. 'The man who we believed murdered Sandra Tupper on this spot less than twenty hours ago, phoned a newspaper, giving the code name he has chosen and which I am not at liberty to divulge to you, and told us he put the murder weapon, a hammer, into the yellow privet by the murder site.' He pointed to the yellow privet. 'That's the only yellow privet I can see, unless you can see any more.' The sergeant and constables looked around them. One or two murmured, 'No, sir.' Hennessey continued. 'Right . . . please search the privet carefully and thoroughly. I don't have to tell you not to touch the hammer, should you see it. If you find it, indicate. I, and I alone will extract it.' Hennessey pointedly snapped on a pair of latex gloves. 'And I, and I alone, will place it in the productions bag. All clear?'

'Yes, sir.' Repeated many times.

Less than ten minutes later DCI Hennessey was in possession of the murder weapon, a balled, or ball-pein hammer, as predicted by Dr D'Acre, and clearly covered with congealed blood.

Somerled Yellich, having accepted the offer of a mug of tea from the remorseful Holly Magg, listened patiently as she recounted what details she could of the man who had quietly slipped into her life, ruined it, then quietly slipped out again.

'Mr X,' she said, 'the name he gave was doubtless an alias. Well, local, but not local to York, Yorkshire accent alright, but it wasn't York, couldn't place it. Yorkshire alright, but not the Vale of York.'

'Hull? Leeds?'

'Could be . . . not the Vale is all I can say.'

'Appearance? Distinguishing features?'

'Short . . . stocky . . . very, very strong . . . very muscular. Thighs like telegraph poles. Clean-shaven, hair cut short, very short, like a skinhead, almost completely shaved. Now, of course, he could be quite hippy-like – he wasn't balding, you see. Distinguishing features . . . top front teeth missing.'

'That could be useful.'

'Green eyes.'

'OK. Occupation?'

'He said he worked for his brother . . . as a driver . . . hence his van.'

'His brother,' Yellich wrote on his pad. 'So, if that was true, he's got family. Where did he live?'

'Again, he never said . . . outside the famous and faire though. He just smelled strongly of the soil sometimes and sometimes there was really heavy duty tools in the back of the van, more than a suburban gardener would need, and his strong wellington boots were thick with mud.'

'I am astounded you got to know so little about him.'

'I am astounded I let him anywhere near me, but he had this softly forceful way and I never had had much success with men before, or since for that matter. The combination of the two . . . and . . . here I am. A terrible disappointment to my family and looking like a very long-term resident of lovely Tang Hall, where the tourists do not visit.'

'Is it too much to hope you have anything containing his DNA or fingerprints?'

'I think it is. It's been years now. I cleaned every-thing out of my old house and anything of his, well there was precious little, anything that was his or even asso-ciated with him I threw out, I was cleansing myself.'

'I can understand that.'

'It was not dissimilar to being raped, except it was my mind, not my body.' She paused as if reliving some suddenly remembered incident, then shuddered. 'Frankly, Mr Yellich, the only reliable things I can tell you about that man is what I saw. I now doubt the truth of anything he told me.'

'But what you saw, what you noticed, is still important . . . missing top front teeth, stocky build, rural living, possibly, Yorkshire accent but not Yorkshire from the Vale.'

'Oh, and an annoying habit of saying "three bad" instead of "too bad". I have heard it often, the children at school used it, and he had picked up the habit . . . might have lost it by now, these silly fads come and go.'

'Three bad?'

'Haven't you heard it used?' Holly Magg smiled briefly.

'No.' Yellich thought it was good she could manage even a brief smile.

'Well, if someone asks, "How are you?" The other person, instead of saying, "Not too bad," replies, "Not three bad." "How did things go?" "Oh, not three bad, thanks."'

'I see.' He added the observation to his notes. 'Yes, that could be annoying.'

'It was especially so when I asked him not to use the expression . . . I didn't know much about human psychology . . . that just made him use it all the more often.'

'You must have been a patient woman.'

'Patient or desperate. Perhaps those women who refuse to compromise are correct after all . . . none of them will get into this mess. I am still nearer the beginning than the end, yet this is my existence now and also my future, sitting in my little flat on this estate, watching the seasons change . . . all because I was bowled over when a man smiled at me in a pub.'

Sergeant Pontefract sat down in front of the television screen and invited Hennessey to sit down in the vacant chair next to him as he slid the video cassette into the

VCR. The 'snow' on the television screen cleared and the image of the foyer at York Station appeared in fast-forward mode with members of the public seeming to scurry in fast forward across the screen. The time and day were shown in the bottom right-hand corner. 'We keep this camera stationary in this position, unless something is happening, in which case we pan and zoom in on to the incident . . . but the phone box is that one there.' Pontefract tapped the screen.

'Clear as day,' said Hennessey.

'So what time did your man make the call?'

'About ten forty a.m. . . . . can't be more precise.'

'We change the tape about six a.m. There is those few seconds when the tape is being replaced that won't be recorded of course.'

'Of course.'

'But they're four-hour tapes on extended play, giving us nearly eight hours of recording, so ten forty this forenoon will be towards the middle of this tape.' Pontefract pressed the 'stop' button then the 'fast forward' and Hennessey heard the tape whirring in the machine.

'Never had time for these things,' Hennessey said.

'Really?' Sergeant Pontefract – crisp white shirt, serge trousers – turned and smiled. 'Couldn't run my household without mine. Stops the children arguing about what programme to watch because one can be watched and the other taped; the rock music show can be switched off when guests arrive, because it can be taped. When I was a lad, the television went off when guests arrived. I can still remember how unfair it felt. My children calmly switch the set off when told to in the knowledge that they can watch the programme when the "dull oldies" have gone.'

'That's useful,' Hennessey nodded. 'I tend to think

136

they encourage people to watch twenty-four-hour television . . . numbs the brain. I read each evening, I just belong to the pre-video and pre-computer era.'

Pontefract stopped the tape. 'This should be about it. Yes, life changing can be difficult if you don't or can't change with it, but the VCR is something I have happily adapted to. Right . . . nine a.m. . . . so let's fast forward from here to ten forty by the timer on the tape. Any indication of his likely age or appearance?'

'None at all . . . male though, strong local accent, so not likely to be of professional middle-class appearance and possibly . . . well, no . . . I was going to assume age, but I can't do that.'

'A bit dangerous, but no need, with this equipment we can freeze-frame and copy the image. We'll do that for every likely person that uses the phone. Not many use payphones, everybody's got those wretched mobiles . . . that is one change I won't adapt to. Can't go on a railway journey now without hearing one half of somebody's conversation. Ten thirty-eight . . . we'll play at normal speed . . .'

'Yes, it's only amusing if they're arguing.'

Pontefract laughed. 'I've never been there, but yes, I can imagine . . . Hello, what's this?'

Both men watched the telvision screen as a tall-looking male in a suit picked up the phone, put money in the slot and dialled a number.

'Not the image I had expected,' Hennessey said, 'but we'll see.'

The man talked for a moment, put the handset down and turned towards the camera as he walked away from the phone. Pontefract froze the screen.

'Nice, sharp image.' Hennessey commented as Pontefract printed the image on to a sheet of paper.

'Can't always guarantee that quality, but they can be

enhanced, you ought to get a good likeness one way or the other.' He handed Hennessey the print. 'Probably not the man . . . too businessman-like, but it's number one.' Both men sat in silence, watching the screen of the monitor in the surveillance suite of the British Transport Police at York railway station, which, when new in the mid-nineteenth century, Hennessey had once read, boasted the largest roof in the world.

'And here,' Pontefract broke the silence as he pressed the 'play' button on the remote, causing the tape to play at normal speed, 'is number two, I think . . . yes, he's going to make a phone call. That, as you see, was at ten forty hours this forenoon.'

Hennessey looked at the figure, short, squat, muscular looking, peaked cap, jacket collar turned up, denims, heavy duty footwear. 'That's our man.'

'You think so?'

'Yes . . . in my waters. He's playing with us, you see, he's taunting us. He must know about the possibility, indeed the probability of CCTV surveillance, yet he uses that payphone, not one in a village out in the sticks where CCTV hasn't yet been invented. He protects himself, that baseball cap, that collar turned up, yet he's not out of doors.'

'I see what you mean.'

'If I was a betting man, I'd lay good money that when he turns away, he'll keep his head down.'

'That's a bet I wouldn't take,' Pontefract growled. 'You're right, if it is your man, he's taunting us.'

'Pity it's not in colour.'

'Isn't it . . . ? The expense we are told is prohibitive but dark cap . . . might get a logo if he turns around, light-coloured jacket . . . it's a scarf, his collar isn't turned up, it's a scarf he's got round his neck.'

'So it is.'

'Feeding coins in, it must be a long-distance call.'

'It was . . . to Dorset.' Hennessey paused, then asked, 'When?'

'Too late.' Pontefract turned to Hennessey. 'You're thinking of lifting his latents from the coins, the same print will only be on so many coins.'

'Yes, I was.'

'British Telecom empties the phones at midday each day, except Sundays and Bank Holidays.'

'Pity.'

'Yes. It would have been useful, especially if he's already known.'

'Useful's not the word . . . if he is already known . . . but useful if he is not and he may have been aware about the time the coins are collected from the payphones. It's the sort of game he'd play. I'm beginning to get into his mind. Making a phone call knowing, at least assuming, he will be caught on CCTV, so hiding his face as much as he can and making the call knowing he's leaving his prints on probably a dozen 20p pieces but also giving us just over an hour to recover them. Such brinkmanship.'

'It's as though he wants to be caught.'

'He does, he has said as much, he is saying as much in that conversation. He just can't give himself up, or stop, but he wants to be caught and so leaves clues wherever he goes.'

'Aye.' Pontefract leaned back in his chair though keeping his eyes on the screen. 'I have heard that . . . aye . . . He's done.'

Hennessey and Pontefract watched the screen as the figure turned to his right, towards the camera, and just as Hennessey predicted, he kept his head down.

Pontefract froze the frame. 'There's a logo on that cap.'

'There is, isn't there? Not clear though. Can you enlarge the image?'

'I can't, not with this equipment, not here. It can be enlarged for you, or enhanced, as I believe the term is, not a problem.'

'If you could . . . we'll need a copy of this for evidence.'

'Again, not a problem.'

'And he terminated the call at ten forty-eight. It's him. BT recorded the call as being received at ten forty. The person who received it said it was a long call . . . eight minutes approximately is a long phone call for a call of that nature.'

'Well, there's a lot you can obtain from that.' Pontefract pressed 'play' and the two officers watched as the man, the person who was by then more than the chief suspect – he was known to be the caller to the *Wimborne Clarion* – walked out of the foyer of the railway station and exited the station. 'Which is where we lose him. We don't have a camera outside the station, we want one but the budget won't run to it.' He rewound the tape and 'froze' it at the point where the man turned away from the phone. 'You can work out his height . . . not a tall lad . . . about five feet six inches, almost one hundred and seventy centimetres in metric.'

'Yes, looks about that. Can you print that off, please?' Pontefract did so.

Hennessey glanced at his watch. 'Won't be able to get the local papers with this until Monday now. We can give it to the local television stations though. Well, thanks, this has helped.' Hennessey stood. 'Onwards and upwards.'

Hennessey walked back to Micklegate Bar Police Station, a mere five-minute stroll from the railway station up curving and inclining Queen Street on a gloomy,

140

drizzle-laden evening. In the police station he found Yellich writing in the 'Bag of Bones' file.

'Late working?' Hennessey stood on the threshold of Yellich's office and smiled approvingly.

'One of those cases, skipper.' Yellich put the pen down. 'That woman's been without food for over two full days now, she'll be getting very hungry and she'll be frightened. Least I can do is to put in a few extra hours.'

'Good man. You've clearly had a productive day.'

'Yes, skipper.' And Yellich told him about the visit to Holly Magg, and the suspect's age and appearance and missing teeth, adding that she agreed to come to the station to provide a 'CD-fit' composite.

'Not bad.' Hennessey reached inside his coat and extracted the print of the frozen frame of the CCTV footage. He dropped it on Yellich's desk. 'It's our man. Definitely. Definitely.'

'He's hiding himself and showing himself at the same time.'

Martin Welsh was 92 years old. He lived alone in a pensioner's flat. He craved company. When there was a gentle tap on his door at the beginning of what he knew was going to be another long and lonely evening with just the television for company, he rose slowly, but eagerly, from his chair to his front door. He hoped for a bit of company and folk occasionally called. He opened the door with a ready smile and received a murderous fist in his face. The intruder stepped over his body, dragged it a few feet into the flat and closed the door. He left the dazed and groaning Martin Welsh on the floor and went to the kitchenette looking for a plastic bag. Having found what he was looking for, he walked out of the kitchen just as an item appeared on the regional

141

news warning the public, 'that the man sought in connection with the "Bag of Bones" murders is believed to be responsible for the death of Sandra Tupper, whose body was found on waste ground in Holgate this morning.' The presenter went on to say that the police warned people, especially young women, 'not to venture out alone at night until this man is caught'. The photograph of the man as he walked away from the payphone in the foyer of York Station was then shown on the screen as believed to be that of the murderer. 'Anyone recognizing this person should contact the police immediately.'

'Close,' said the man, 'but not close enough, and who said anything about young women out of doors?' After he had placed the plastic bag over Martin Welsh's head he turned and sifted through items and articles on the sideboard in the old man's living room and finding a pencil which he thought would do, wrote on the wallpaper above the hearth: 'I told you to stop me'.

It was Saturday. 18.45 hours.

Six

in which a long night is passed and two people have a three-way conversation.

SATURDAY, 19.00 HOURS – SUNDAY, 04.00 HOURS

Yellich put the phone down and sat back in his chair. It wasn't the first time he had made such a phone call and he doubted that it would be the last. Again, Sara had been good about it, understanding that a police officer cannot punch a time clock at predetermined hours. She understood the need to have to work late when occasion demands and again, her only concern was how Jeremy would take the news that his father would be home too late tonight to spend time with him. She said she would do her best, 'but he's getting unmanageable these days'. Somerled Yellich knew he had a very, very good wife, who, he felt, deserved more than he could give. He considered himself a fortunate man. Then his phone rang. He snatched it up. 'DS Yellich.'

'Lady to speak to you, sir.' The switchboard operator's voice was calm, efficient. 'Miss Magg.'

'Oh, yes . . . put her through, please.'

There was a pause, a silence, the line clicked, then a female voice said, 'Hello?'

'Miss Magg?'

'Yes . . . is that Mr Yellich?'

143

'Yes, it is.'

'You visited me today, about Mr Carpenter.'

Mr Carpenter, Yellich sighed, the man ruined her life yet she can still call him Mr Carpenter. 'Yes, I did . . . I remember, of course I remember.'

'Well, I've seen the news, the local news . . .'

'Yes?'

'And I have a copy of the evening paper . . .'

'Yes?'

'Well, the footage of the man making the phone call, at the railway station.'

'Yes?'

'It's definitely David Carpenter . . . that walk . . . the way he carries himself, even though his face can't be seen, I tell you that's him alright.'

'You're certain?'

'As certain as can be. If it isn't him, he's got a double in this city.'

'Well, thanks, Miss Magg. We don't know him by the way, not as David Carpenter, so that might be an alias, as you indicated it might be.'

'I recalled something else.'

'Oh?'

'He'd been in prison.'

'He had?' Yellich leaned forwards and gripped the phone.

'Well, so he told me and for some reason, it is the one thing, perhaps one of the things, I believed.'

'Well, if he was in prison, then that confirms that David Carpenter is an alias. What did he tell you? Anything you can remember?'

'He said he was in Armley.'

'Leeds?'

'Is that where it is?'

'Yes. Looks like a castle dominating the skyline to the south of the city.'

'Oh . . . He did three months for theft.'

'So he said?'

'Yes . . . so he said, but it didn't seem like a boast or some gesture of contrition to get in my good books, so I believed him. I just did. Call it woman's intuition if you want to.'

'Do you know when he was in Armley? At least when he said he was in there?'

'Just before he and I met. So that would be about five or six years ago.'

'I see . . . helps us age him. So he's at least twenty-six years of age?'

'More . . . he's in his thirties, that I can tell you. He's been in my bed, remember.'

'Yes . . . yes . . . green eyes, missing front teeth and an annoying habit of saying "not three bad". Sorry, I was thinking aloud when I mentioned his age.'

'I see. So he's wanted in connection with that woman who disappeared?'

'Yes, and a few other matters.'

'Well, if he's got a farm he can keep her pretty well undetected, but only if he lives alone, or only if anyone he lives with is in on it all. Have you thought of that?'

'Yes . . . thanks for the observation, Miss Magg.' Yellich shook his head and thought: Once a teacher, always a teacher. 'It's something we'll bear in mind.'

'OK. If I remember anything, I'll phone you. I ask for you . . . yes?'

'Or DCI Hennessey . . . either.'

'Alright.' She put the phone down, gently so.

Yellich too replaced his receiver and reached for the file on the disappearance of Mrs Handy as cross-referenced to the 'Bag of Bones' file and recorded Miss Magg's information about the identity of the man in the CCTV footage. After writing 'Armley for 3/12 5/6/12 ago' he wrote 'David Carpenter – used as an alias' and then added 'smallholding?' It was, he thought, quite a valid point. After all a man could live on a smallholding and live alone, enabling him to hold a person against their will. Anything larger, even the smallest of farms, would be likely to be worked by a family or with the help of farm hands. He stood and walked to Hennessey's office and reported the contents of the phone call he had received from Holly Magg.

'A smallholding?' Hennessey raised an eyebrow. 'That's an interesting notion. It could narrow the field down a little.'

'Need more to go on, this guy is phoning newspapers all over the UK. Alright, he phoned from York Station, but he could still be anywhere . . . Have van, will travel.'

'Somehow I don't think he's too far away, Yellich, my waters tell me he's not too far away at all. There're too many local connections, he's local, his accent, he was involved with a locally living lady . . . Miss Magg.'

'Yes.'

'He's probably been in Armley. That's a local nick, as you know.'

'Yes . . . and he abducted locally . . . Henry Fulwood and now Mrs Handy. He's local alright. I'll bet a half an hour's car drive from here. We're closing down on him, Yellich.'

'Wish I was as confident as you, skipper. I feel we are groping in the dark.'

'We're close.' Hennessey smiled. 'Close, close . . . close. You'd better tell the press officer about his alias, David Carpenter. Someone might know him by that name.'

'Very good, boss. Consider it done.'

'You're working late?'

'Didn't want to go home, sir. Mrs Handy out there being starved to death, I'd feel guilty being at home, eating home cooking.'

146

'I know what you mean. I feel the same, but there's little we can do. No witnesses to the Sandra Tupper murder have come forward. Alert the press officer to the alias, then get home.'

'Sara would appreciate that, sir.' Yellich smiled his thanks. 'Our Jeremy's getting a bit much for her. You know he's a big lad for twelve, but only about four years old in his head. Like any woman, she could handle a four-year-old but a twelve-year-old four-year-old . . .'

'Yes, I understand. You should be at home. Look upon it as rest and recuperation . . . You, me, none of us will be any good to anyone if we collapse with exhaustion. I'm doing the same. You don't mind coming in tomorrow, Sunday? It's your day off.'

'No, sir. I'll be in.'

'Good man. I'll be here too.'

Hennessey drove home to Easingwold. Night had fallen. The drizzle was blown sideways. He thought how the weather can turn a pleasant drive into a lonely road. He reached Easingwold and his detached house on the Thirsk Road and turned into the driveway. He walked quickly from his car to the house, which he entered by the front door. He was greeted warmly by his brown mongrel who barked excitedly and turned in tight circles with a vigorous wagging of his tail. Hennessey responded by bending down and patting his dog's head and neck and telling the animal that he was 'a good dog' – 'good dog, good dog, Oscar' – 'good dog' for man and dog had developed a bond which was as strong, if not stronger than, the emotional bonds which develop between humans. Hennessey walked to his kitchen, where he made himself a mug of tea which he carried to the back door. He opened the back door and, unwilling to venture into the garden because of the rain, he began to talk.

'Odd sort of day,' he said, 'busy but little sense of progress. Another murder last night, which we have linked to the "Bag of Bones" murders. DS Yellich interviewed a woman who has badly messed up her life, but she did give us information. There is the sense that we are closing down on the perp, but at the same time, he's eluding us . . . and all the while his captive . . . the woman he has abducted, is being starved of food, in this weather too. I hope for her sake she's indoors, in shelter with some source of warmth. Going hungry when you're cold is no fun, the human body needs food to withstand heat loss.'

An observer would see a middle-aged man talking to himself. If an observer did make that reasonable assumption, of a man a little 'wandered' in his head, and if George Hennessey knew that assumption had been made about him then, dear reader, it is doubtful that he would be concerned. Each day, when at home, usually in the early evening upon returning from work, he would go into the garden, or, as on this occasion, stand on the threshold of the back door, and tell his beloved wife, who has not grown old as he that is left had grown old, about his day. Earlier that year, in the mid-summer, he had told her of a new love in his life, and had assured her that it did mean that his love for her was diminished but he hoped that she understood his need and upon saying that, had experienced a strange warmth cloaking him which he could not explain by the sun's rays alone.

His present lady had come into his life only recently. She had still to meet his son and was keen to do so, though he had met her, younger, children. They had early on agreed strict rules of protocol, for their paths occasionally crossed during their working day. He reflected that on a day-to-day basis his relationships were both largely abstract: one was with a woman who would always be his lovely, lovely young wife . . . and the other with a woman whom he had also come to love but whom he saw only briefly – an occasional night together or even more occasionally, when their schedules allowed them, an escape to a hotel in another town for two or three days and nights by themselves. Strange, he pondered, strange that he could be in love with two women but despite that, most mornings he wakes up alone.

George Hennessey returned inside his house and prepared a meal, a grilled steak garnished with onions and potatoes, with a thick, garlic-flavoured gravy – just the one wholesome course as is 'survival' cooking. Upon clearing away the dishes, he settled down in front of an open fire and read further of a scholarly work analysing the Battle of Monte Cassino. He had purchased the piece for his collection of military history some years earlier and had been reluctant to start reading it, being daunted by its length and loftiness, but once started, he would soldier on until he had completed it. Later still, after reading for two hours, Hennessey gave Oscar his main meal of the day and dragged the reluctant mongrel into the rain, insisting on their normal one-mile walk. Upon returning home, Oscar shook the rain indignantly from his coat, pleasing Hennessey that his dog felt secure enough to be angry. Hennessey then strolled in the slightly easing rain into Easingwold, for a pint of stout at the Dove Inn, just one, before 'last orders' were called.

'I know that man.' Yellich spoke softly, his arm round his wife's shoulders as she curled up next to him on the settee. The late-evening regional news had shown the footage of the man wanted in connection with the 'Bag of Bones' murders and the abduction of Mrs Handy as he walked across the concourse of York railway station.

This time, the commentary added that the police have announced that the man is believed to use the alias 'David Carpenter'.

'You know him?' Sara Yellich turned to her husband.

'Yes . . . I mean, I have seen him, looking at it again . . . somewhere . . . I have seen him, not too long ago either. Not too long ago at all.'

Linda Handy raised her head involuntarily at the sound of his van; it was a sound she had come to recognize and towards which she had developed an ambivalence of emotion. She was frightened of the man, but being in the house alone also frightened her. She could, under normal circumstances, cope with being alone; in fact she quite enjoyed solitude as an occasional welcome break from her family and its demands. But the house frightened her: it was a building in which a great deal of pain of all sorts had been experienced. Twelve people had been starved to death within these walls, and she began to harbour expectations that she would indeed become number thirteen as hope slipped steadily away with each passing hour, indeed each passing minute. She believed that buildings assume the emotions experienced within them. She had sensed a warm and happy atmosphere in one or two empty houses on the occasions in her life when she had been house hunting, and equally, on such occasions, she had felt a coldness in houses she had viewed on hot, sun-filled days, or a tension or a high level of stress about her when the only other person present was an enthusiastic estate agent, keen to make the sale proceed. She looked about her. This house, this modest, unassuming, small house, had clearly absorbed much that made it deeply uncomfortable to be in alone for Linda Handy, over and above her predicament and her uncertain future. It was a cold and, atmospherically speaking, she felt it to be a badly damaged building. Thus, even the presence of her abductor had a strangely attractive quality. She listened as the man alighted from the van, and shut the door with a bang. No neighbours to worry about here was the clear message she believed that he was transmitting by slamming the vehicle's door with such force, as was the loud sound of his heavy footwear crunching the gravel outside his house as he walked the short distance from the van to his front door. He unlocked just a single lock, clearly, she thought, fearing no burglary in his absence and further reinforcing the impression she had developed that wherever this house was with its dreadful history, it was in a remote place. A very remote place indeed. She listened as the man walked towards the room she was in and shut her eyes at the anticipation of the sudden dazzle as he switched on the electric light.

'Good evening?' she asked with eyes clenched shut.

'Not bad.' He peeled off his jacket and flung it over a chair, as she slowly opened her eyes, keeping her head bent down, away from the light source. 'I've had better Saturday nights.'

She remained silent. I've had better Saturday nights. She pondered his response, it implied self-employment.

'Not three bad . . . but I've had better.'

'Good, that's the nature of business, it goes up and down.'

'Yes,' he sat heavily on to the settee, 'these salaried folk . . . money coming in each month, like clockwork.'

She smiled to herself – so he *is* self-employed. Any information about him would be useful in the unlikely event of her escaping or being chanced upon in his absence.

'You'll be working soon.'

'I will?'

'Aye . . . Wales . . . think of a small town in Wales.'

'Well ... Monmouth,' she offered. 'How about Monmouth?'

'Yes ... I like that ... Monmouth.' He opened the take-away kebab he had clearly just purchased. The smell of hot food assailed, assaulted, attacked her senses. She didn't react. She didn't want to give him the satisfaction of seeing her anguish. She made another deduction. His house was not evidently so remote after all, if he could return home with a takeaway meal which upon his arrival was still clearly hot enough to eat there and then without having to be reheated in the oven. Hope re-emerged. There came the sense that help was out there, and not so far off after all.

'Getting hungry?' he asked, forcing the chips and chicken and pitta bread into his mouth.

'Wasn't that the idea?'

'Nope.'

'No? What *was* the idea?'

'To kill you slowly ... your hunger is incidental. If we could find another way of killing you slowly, we would ... but we like this method.'

'We?'

'I ... we ... what difference does it make?' He became angry, his voice suddenly had a hard edge.

'So, why Wales?' Linda Handy changed the subject rapidly.

'I'll be making a phone call tomorrow.'

'To a newspaper?'

'Yes ... you see we killed again tonight.'

She felt as if she had been kicked in the stomach. She became too frightened to speak. He would tell her what he ... what 'they' wanted her to know.

'Yeah ... it was Tony what done it.'

'Tony?'

'Yeah,' the man said warmly and instantly his voice

152

changed to become hard, snarling. 'I'm Tony.'

A chill shot down the woman's spine. 'Tony . . .' she ventured.

'What?' Again the voice was hard.

'Just saying "hi". Haven't met you before.'

'No . . . So what . . . ? You're going to die, bitch, anyway.'

'Slowly . . . I've been told.'

'Yeah, that was Horace's idea. He's soft but he has good ideas, then it's me that has to carry them through. It was me that said we needed another victim, keep the pressure up on the police. Chose an old guy in sheltered housing, just steamed in . . . I did the business and then Horace took over. It's always Horace that picks up after us . . . so he'll be phoning someone tomorrow.'

'Tomorrow?' She paused. 'Is it Saturday or Sunday today? I have lost track.'

'Oh . . . that's right.' He tossed her a chip and piece of chicken. She snatched them up and ate them hurriedly. 'Horace doesn't like me doing that, but me, I'm doing you no favour, I'm keeping you alive longer see . . . prolonging the agony . . . but Horace doesn't see it like that. He's a bit weak, Horace is, weak . . . but yeah . . . you're right, Saturday. Have to phone on Monday, tell them it was us who did for the old boy.'

There was a silence. The man continued to eat the kebab.

'Shouldn't be doing this.' The voice was soft, concerned.

'Horace?' Handy ventured.

'Who told you my name?'

'Tony.'

'You've been speaking to Tony?'

'Yes.'

'You shouldn't, Tony is dangerous, you don't want to mess with Tony.'

'He spoke to me . . . I wasn't messing with him.'

'You don't even want to speak to him, see. He told you my name, he's careless. I have to clean up after us, after he's done the business. It was Tony who sprayed Mace in your face.'

'Is that what it was? I've heard of Mace . . . never knew what it was,' she said to draw him out.

'I have a cousin in America, he sends it to me. Tony liked it, he said it would be useful for us. He was right. We didn't always have Mace, that's why all the others were also women, except one guy. Tony took a real dislike to the guy . . . the whistling milkman . . . rattling the bottles early in the morning, waking him up when he was staying at his girlfriend's. Tony takes a dislike to somebody, that somebody better watch out . . . I mean watch out. So don't talk to Tony if you know what's best for you.'

'OK,' she spoke softly, 'that's good advice. Thank you, Horace.'

The man grunted.

'Horace?' She was testing the waters.

'Yes?'

'Horace . . . do you think what Tony is doing is right? I mean what you and Tony are doing. Do you think it's right?'

'No.' The voice remained soft. 'No, it's not right . . . not right.' The man looked towards the window. 'Out there, there's twelve people . . . planted . . . and trees planted over them. They shouldn't have been murdered, no, it's not right.' He picked unenthusiastically at the kebab. Like, she thought, a man eating because he knows he has to eat, rather than because he wants to eat. 'I want us to be caught. We can't go on doing this.'

'So why go on?'

He looked at her as if astounded by her question.

'Because Tony says so, he's the boss . . . do you see? He's in charge. I do what Tony tells me. Tony would be angry, he'd be furious if I didn't go along with his plan.'

'I'd help you, I'd protect you.' She held the chain that bound her to the wall. 'Release me from this, I'll make sure Tony won't get you.'

The man smiled. 'You're trying to trick me and anyway, Tony warned me about you playing tricks. He said, they'll all play tricks, they always do, Tony said. I have to do what Tony says. Where would we go anyway?'

'Somewhere we'd both be safe from Tony.'

'Somewhere like what?'

'Like a police station, Horace, we'll both be safe from Tony in a police station.'

The man fell silent. Hope rose in the woman. Then the man looked at her with cold, piercing eyes, eyes she had come to learn belonged to Tony. 'Stop your tricks,' the man snarled. 'You leave Horace alone, you leave him well alone, hear? Stay well clear of him.' He tossed her a piece of meat. 'I told you I'll feed you a little – Horace won't at all. You mess about with Horace again and you won't even get that.'

'But it's only to prolong the agony, you said that. So why should I worry about not getting any food?' although she pushed the piece of meat into her mouth in a rapid, desperate manner.

'At least it prolongs it. Could make a difference between an extra few days of life; that could mean a difference on whether you survive or not. The blue bogies might find you in time. You want to be rescued, don't you?'

'Yes, of course I want to be rescued, I've got a family.'

'Well, eat what I give you but don't tell Horace . . . it'll vex him. I have to look after Horace, he's not strong like me. I don't want him vexed. Understand?'

'Yes,' said meekly as she probed the gaps between her

teeth with her tongue tip, hoping to find any small, slightest sliver of meat which might have become lodged therein.

The man finished the kebab, now eating angrily, jabbing the food into his mouth. Having finished the meal, he collected the wrapping of the carryout and left the room, switching off the light as he did so.

Linda Handy pulled the blanket around her as, outside, an owl hooted. She leaned back against the wall. So nobody knew where she was, but what she did know was that she was within an easy car drive of a kebab shop: that could mean as little as a fifteen-minute walk. She felt at the chain. It was solid, too solid to pull free of the place where it was attached, and the padlock which held it fastened round her ankle was also solid. She wouldn't be able to free herself. But she had to help herself some way; she had to make a determined contri- bution to her survival. The man was mad, as clear a split personality as she had ever read about, at least two personalities were in there – 'Horace' meek and ques- tioning, prone to guilt, but frightened of 'Tony', who was the dangerous one. If she was going to do anything to help herself, she reasoned, it would have to be by cultivating a relationship with meek and guilty-feeling Horace.

She probed her teeth with her tongue in another vain attempt to find a little food. With a remnant of humour, she thought her attempt to find food lodged in-between her teeth was akin to an angler standing on the bank of a river, yelling at unseen fish to take his bait, and in a further glimmer of dark humour, she thought she might even have time to work on 'Horace', to bring him round to her thinking – after all, she had been reliably informed that she had about a month to do it in. She lowered herself down and lay on the floor, picking out objects in the gloom, hoping for sleep as an escape, but that night, sleep, with all its cruelty, evaded her and thoughts and memories and regrets, especially her life's regrets, whirled incessantly round her mind like taunting demons.

Sleep also evaded George Hennessey. Thoughts also whirled about his mind and his regrets also emerged to haunt him, often playing like a video loop, reliving the incident, getting to the end, then starting at the beginning again, over and over and over, as he too heard an owl hoot somewhere outside his house, though close to his house – the orchard, he thought, about that sort of distance. Then, although at the rear of his house, and sleeping with open curtains because his bedroom looked out on to the open country beyond the bottom of his garden, he heard a motorcycle roar at speed along the Thirsk Road and that sound reached deeply into George Hennessey's soul.

Upon hearing the sound, he was transported in his memory back to his childhood home in Greenwich, at the bottom end of Trafalgar Road on the way to struggling Plumstead, and the memory of his older brother, Graham, with his beloved Triumph, and again knowing the truth of the observation that a man or woman is not measured by the hole they fill when they die, but by the hole they leave behind them.

George Hennessey lay still, turned on his side, lay still, turned on his other side, until the sky above his home grew lighter as a new day was dawning and then sleep, lovely, lovely sleep, mercifully rescued him from torment.

In Holgate, Pearl Tupper sat at her bedroom window looking out over the backs of the houses as the dawn broke, causing the slate roofs of the outhouses to gleam. Sleep also evaded her, but unlike George Hennessey, it evaded her because she was getting hungry, really quite hungry by then, and she didn't know who was going to the shops for her, now her daughter was no more.

Seven

in which yet another victim is claimed.

SUNDAY, 10.00 HOURS – 22.00 HOURS

George Hennessey arrived at Micklegate Bar Police Station at 10 a.m., signed in and walked to the CID corridor to find Yellich at his desk, writing up a file. He tapped on the doorframe of Yellich's office. 'Sorry I'm late in.'

'Skipper!' Yellich sat back and smiled.

'Had a dreadful night, just couldn't get to sleep, must have been four this morning before I nodded off . . . woke at nine . . . felt refreshed. It's not the length of sleep but the quality.'

'So I have found too, skipper. Remember once . . .' Yellich stood and walked to the corner of his office where stood an electric kettle, mugs, tea and coffee and a carton of milk, 'some years back now . . . I was still in uniform.' He checked the level of water in the kettle and switched it on. 'The first nightshift in a run . . . got up at ten a.m. that day, lazed about conserving energy, reported for duty at ten p.m. Coffee?'

'Tea if you have it, please.' Hennessey sat in the chair in front of Yellich's desk.

'Had to attend court the next day to give evidence, so that when I reported to the Crown Court that morning, I

159

had already been without sleep for twenty-four hours, wasn't called and was dismissed at five p.m. so . . . work it out . . . by then thirty-one hours without sleep. I was getting confused, speaking gibberish, I was told. Fortunately someone drove me home. Collapsed into bed and surprised nobody more than myself by waking in time to start the next nightshift at ten p.m. . . . Four hours sleep but utterly refreshed after it. So, as you say, boss, it's not the length of sleep, but the quality.' The kettle boiled and he poured the water into the small metal teapot into which he had dropped a single teabag. 'Mind, it's not an experience I would care to repeat and I shudder to think what sort of witness I would have made if I had been called at about four p.m. that day. The possibility that that could easily have happened has a place on my haunting pile.' He poured the tea and handed the mug to Hennessey.

'Yes, it's often the case.' Hennessey grasped the mug with both hands. 'Thanks. It's often the case that the thought of what could easily have happened but didn't is harder to live with than actual events, events which did happen, because with events that did happen, you are coping with a finality . . . With potentially tragic things that didn't happen but could so easily have happened, you are left with an infinity of imagination.'

'Harder to live with, as you say, skipper, sometimes anyway.' Yellich returned to his chair. 'Dare say it depends on the actuality of the awful thing itself.'

'Dare say . . . but I understand your insecurity when pondering what sort of witness you would have made had you been called after thirty hours without sleep. So . . . today . . . the here and now, with Mrs Handy, now approaching a third full day without food . . . if ye Dance Master is to be believed . . . and I tend to believe him.'

'So do I, skipper, so do I.'

'Nobody saw anything of the Sandra Tupper murder,

nobody has come forward anyway. You checked our records for David Carpenter?'

'Yes, boss . . . not a thing . . . Didn't think there would be, frankly.'

'Neither did I, frankly.' Hennessey sipped his tea. 'This is good.' He smiled. 'First tea of the day. I piled out of the house without breakfast.'

'Not a good idea, boss, especially in winter.'

'Aye . . . just made sure my best pal had enough water in his bowl and a few biscuits, then left the house, pulling my coat on as I did so. So this is more than welcome.'

'No worries, boss, but as you say, this is looking like a cul de sac,' Yellich paused. 'But having said that . . . having said that . . .'

'Yes?' Hennessey allowed a note of hope to enter his voice.

'Well, as I said to our Sara last night – I watched the CCTV of the Dance Master walking across the concourse of York Station – I have seen that guy, I tell you I have seen him . . . and recently too . . . just can't place him.'

'Oh . . .' Hennessey groaned. 'I know what you mean, again, I know what you mean . . . but you don't need me to tell you the importance of this.'

'I know, sir, I know. I hesitated about telling you, unless I suddenly remembered, but that walk . . .'

'So it was somewhere outside that you saw him?'

'Probably.'

'And by recently . . . how recent is "recent"?'

'Boss, the agony of this is torturing me.'

'We'll go over your diary, go through your notebook – you'll be able to retrace your steps that way.'

'Yes, boss.' Yellich hadn't thought of that. 'So obvious, but I hadn't thought of it.' He reached for his notebook. 'I'll do that right away.'

Then his phone rang. He picked it up and Hennessey

watched as Yellich's eyebrows furrowed and he turned his notebook to a fresh page and picked up his pen and started to write. 'OK . . . got that . . . we'll be there directly.' He replaced the receiver.

'It's another one, sir.'

'Another what?'

'Murder,' Yellich said solemnly. 'It's another murder. Linked to this.' He patted the 'Bag of Bones' file.

'How do you know?'

'It's got Dance Master written all over it. Literally. The constable reports writing on the wall signed by the "Dance Master".'

'Oh my,' Hennessey sighed. 'Where away?'

'Clouston Court . . . it's a sheltered housing complex . . . elderly people, living alone in self-contained flats, warden on site who checks on each resident once every twenty-four hours. Old boy didn't answer his buzzer . . . they have an intercom connected to the warden's flat. Warden went round with her set of keys . . . found said old boy with a plastic bag over his head, assumed suicide but would have called us anyway . . . suicide being a suspicious death.'

'Yes . . . yes.'

'The old boy was given to mood swings and had depressive phases, so she wasn't too surprised to find what she found, then saw the writing on the wall, called three nines, cops arrived . . . she pointed at the writing.'

'What does it say?' Hennessey stood.

'"Stop us before we do this again . . . Dance Master".'

'"We"?!'

'Yes, boss.' Yellich reached for his coat. '"We" . . . "*We* do this again". Don't know what to make of that "we" . . . We took the "us" in Sylvester's message as vernacular singular, but "we" is unambiguously plural. It's contradictory. And I feel sure we're dealing with one person – not a group.'

'I know, that occurred to me, Yellich.' Hennessey turned and walked out of Yellich's office. Yellich followed closely behind. '"Stop us . . ." "Stop us . . ."' Hennessey repeated as he and Yellich strode down the CID corridor toward the enquiry desk and the exit. '"We do this . . ." You know, if that is sincere and not a calculated attempt to throw us of the scent, it could only mean one thing.'

'A nutter?'

'Well . . . I care not for your turn of phrase, but yes, we are dealing with criminal insanity here, a split personality for which we need to take learned advice. Nevertheless, we'll see what we see.'

Hennessey and Yellich viewed the corpse. Elderly, male, baggy grey trousers, cream cardigan with buttons missing, worn and scuffed carpet slippers. The flat in which he lived was cluttered, piles of newspapers on chairs, inexpensive mementoes from holiday resorts stood atop the sideboard. Both officers thought it was not a pleasant end to a life, a one-bedroom council-owned flat surrounded by trivia, though neither voiced their feelings. They turned their attention to the wall above the fireplace and read the message: 'Stop us before we do this again – Dance Master'. It was written in pencil on the wallpaper.

'Well, we have his handwriting,' Hennessey mused. 'Every little bit counts.'

'Yes, he could have printed it, but he's chosen to let us see his handwriting.' Yellich looked at the writing. 'I think you're right, boss . . .'

'Right?' Hennessey turned to him. 'In what way?'

'Well, a few days ago . . . your notion that he wants to be caught, but for some reason, can't give himself up. He's leaving clues about himself all over the place. It's more than just taunting us, he really does want all this to end.'

'Or part of him does, and that means part of him does not and we have to worry about the part that does not. So, who found him? The warden, you say?'

'Yes, sir. She's the lady who was standing next to the constable as we came in.'

'Alright. If you could wait just outside the door for the police surgeon, I'll go and chat to the warden.'

'Yes, sir.'

Hennessey walked out of the stuffy, difficult-to-breathe flat of the deceased and walked to where a young constable and middle-aged lady stood.

'Clark, isn't it?' Hennessey addressed the constable.

'Yes, sir.'

'You were at Cambridge House a week ago . . . a week ago tomorrow?'

'The "Bag of Bones" case . . . yes, sir, first there for my sins.'

'Well, constables often are first there . . . for their sins. And this is the lady who found the body?'

'Yes. This is Mrs Haden, the warden of the flats.'

Hennessey thought Mrs Haden had a hard, unyielding, emotionless look: cold eyes amid a strong, almost manly face. She held eye contact with Hennessey as if waiting to be interviewed.

'We understand how you found him . . . I mean the process . . . he didn't respond to your call this morning, so you followed it up and found him and called three nines?'

No reply.

'Well . . . ?' Hennessey realized this interview was going to be an uphill battle and regretted not delegating it to Sergeant Yellich.

'You live on the estate, within this complex?'

'Is that a question?' She had a cold voice. She was not at all the sort of woman Hennessey would imagine being appointed to look after the well-being of elderly people.

'Yes, it's a question.'

'Then yes, I do.'

'When did you last see Mr . . .'

'Welsh,' the woman said. 'He is Martin Welsh, bachelor, no known relatives.'

'I see.'

'I have his name, sir,' Constable Clark said. 'I've noted everything that Mrs Haden has been able to tell me about the deceased.'

'Good man.' Hennessey smiled and nodded at PC Clark. He turned back to Mrs Haden, for Mrs she was by the band on her finger. 'When did you last see Mr Welsh alive?'

'Last see him . . . probably two weeks ago, to set eyes on him, but I spoke to him last through the intercom yesterday morning at about ten a.m. I call each resident at about ten. If one doesn't answer, I go out and check on him or her. That's my job. Contact every resident once every twenty-four hours and if they answer the intercom and say they are well, that's it. If they don't answer, I have to check on them. Also I have to respond if they press their alarm button. I have to do that as well. It's a nice, quiet job and will suit me until I draw my pension. Suit me well, so it will.'

'I can imagine. So did you see anyone acting suspiciously in or around Clouston Court in the last day or two?'

'No. Not acting suspiciously.'

'Meaning?'

'Well, a stranger yesterday . . . but he was just walking through the Court, some folk use it as a shortcut . . . you get to know them. I've been doing this job for five years now, so I have, and you get to know the ones who use

the Court to get from the housing estate to the bus route
. . . no reason why they shouldn't, doesn't do any harm,
keeps the Court alive . . . more folk walking through the
better, as many good eyes as can be had.'

'I see.' Hennessey saw a warmer side beginning to
emerge in Mrs Haden's personality.

'Yes . . . stops the wrong sort gathering here . . . the
glue sniffers. We get them but I chase them off. I have a
big dog . . . I take him out . . . he helps.'

'Bet he does.'

'Well, I was out last night, early evening, about six
thirty . . . saw this man . . . he wasn't walking through the
estate, but he came down the stairs. Mr Welsh is on the
first floor, as you see, have to take the stairs to his flat.
Saw this man come down the stairs . . . walked past me
and walked to where he'd parked his van.'

'A van?' Hennessey couldn't help a note of enthusiasm
enter his voice.

'Aye . . . a white van.'

'Any writing on the van?'

'No . . . just a white van. I wouldn't know what type,
I'm afraid – they all look the same to me. I can tell a car
from a van but that's about it, also a motorbike from a
bus. I can tell you that.'

'I see. Did you get a good look at the man?'

'Yes . . . good enough.'

'In that case, we'll have to ask you to go to the station
to compose a CD-fit.'

'If you wish.'

'I wish. What was he wearing?'

'Green jacket, like soldiers wear.'

'A combat jacket . . . camouflaged?'

'Not camouflaged, just drab olive green . . . jeans, heavy
boots, like working boots and gloves.'

'Gloves?'

'Gloves. If he was the murderer, you won't find prints in there . . . not cold enough for gloves last night, but he was wearing them.'

'That's interesting, sounds like we'll need that CD-fit.'

'Alright. He had mad eyes.'

'Mad eyes?'

'Well, they say that eyes are the window to the soul, couldn't see into that one's soul, no way, not a chance. His eyes were glassy, couldn't see into them . . . like looking into a mirror . . . mad eyes, mad, mad eyes.'

'Right. Constable Clark.'

'Sir?'

'Could you please take Mrs Haden to the station, have the police artist compose a CD-fit of the man she saw yesterday evening.'

'You'll bring me home again, I hope?'

'Of course.'

'Police surgeon, sir.' PC Clark indicated to the area behind Hennessey.

'Thanks.' Hennessey turned and saw the turbaned Dr Mann get out of his car, black bag in hand, and ask directions of the constable on the ground in front of the stairs which led to the first-floor landing and to the home of Martin Welsh (deceased).

Hennessey walked to where Yellich stood and PC Clark escorted Mrs Haden to the police car via another set of stairs.

Minutes later Dr Mann stood and said to Hennessey, 'Well, I pronounce life extinct as at ten forty a.m. this day.'

'Ten forty a.m.,' Hennessey repeated as Yellich entered the time in his notebook.

'Death appears to be by suffocation, but I can only say "appears".'

'Understood, Doctor.'

'I assume, because of all the police activity, you are treating this as murder?'

'Yes . . . we are.'

'Not suicide? A plastic bag over one's head is a method of suicide favoured by the elderly.'

'I didn't know that, but no, in this case we have grounds to suspect foul play.'

'Very well.' Dr Mann turned. 'Even on Sundays a policeman's work is never done.'

'Indeed, sir. Thank you for coming out.'

'I had to.' Dr Mann smiled. 'Same as you.'

'Nonetheless, thank you.' Hennessey turned to Yellich as Dr Mann took his leave. 'Can you contact York District Hospital, ask them to contact Dr D'Acre? That's one lady who will object most strongly to having to come out . . . but needs must.'

'Yes, sir.' Yellich reached for his mobile.

'She's a very keen horsewoman, you see.'

'Really, boss?' Yellich pressed a button on his mobile and a pre-keyed number began to ring.

'So I believe. If you've ever been to her study in the hospital . . . photographs of her horse and children abound and she once told me that Sunday is "hacking" day for her and her family. Spend the day at the stables or taking to their horse on short, localized walks.'

'I see, sir.' Yellich held the mobile to his ear. When it was answered he spoke, identified himself and waited to be put through, spoke again and said, 'Thank you.' He switched off his mobile. 'They're contacting her, sir.'

'Thanks.' Hennessey glanced at his watch. 'Ten forty-five . . . they might just catch her. Hope they don't, in a sense, she'll not be best pleased at giving up a day at the stables, I'll be bound, and this can easily be done by whichever pathologist in Harrogate is on call.'

The two men waited in silence. Hennessey looked about

him, the low-rise apartments, in blocks, stood in a grass-covered area surrounded by trees.

'Quiet,' he said.

'Sir?'

'This area . . . very quiet, not a bad place for the elderly.'

'No.' Yellich looked at Clouston Court. 'Rather hope I don't end my days in one of those little boxes.'

'Me neither – nowhere to exercise my dog, even if they let you keep dogs.'

Yellich's phone rang. He answered it, said, 'Thank you.' He switched it off and said, 'Dr D'Acre's on her way, sir.'

Hennessey smiled. 'Oh boy, she won't be a happy lassie . . . not a happy lassie at all.'

The man carried the meal into the room and set it down on the table. He surveyed it with eager anticipation. He looked at the woman. She looked at him and thought: Who are you now? Which one are you today – ruthless Tony or gentle but deeply troubled Horace? Which one?

'I'd give you food,' he said, 'but Tony's told me not to.'

Horace . . . for the moment it was Horace. Horace she could talk to, Horace could be reasoned with. Even if he didn't give her a single scrap of food, she felt safer with Horace than with Tony . . . even though Tony might throw her a little to eat. And even if he was giving her a little to eat so as to prolong her suffering, he was still giving her something, and anything, any tiny morsel of food meant her body didn't have to eat itself of that equivalent amount. She had stopped feeling hungry: her stomach had clearly shrunk all it was going to shrink. Now the danger time begins: the fat reserves will have been used up by now and she was a slender lady and believed that she wouldn't have great reserves anyway . . . now her body would be beginning to eat its muscle; once eaten, that, unlike the fat reserves, cannot be replaced. She knew she had to do something, to say something, yet she also knew that 'Tony' had the ability to make a sudden reappearance. She decided not to risk provoking the dormant 'Tony' and so remained silent.

'Horace' ate his meal in silence. When he had finished, he dropped his knife and fork on the plate and pushed it away from him in a gesture, it seemed, of contempt.

Contempt for food. Linda Handy closed her eyes at witnessing the image. Apart from the disgraceful table manners, she wondered how he could do such a thing, even if she wasn't sitting there, shackled to the wall, drinking all the water she wanted, but not having had any food, save the odd scraps that cruel and contemptuous 'Tony' had thrown to her. He could not only eat a substantial meal, but at the end of it show disdain for what keeps all humans alive.

'Like my Sunday breakfast.' He sat back and patted his stomach. 'Sunday isn't Sunday without a proper breakfast.'

'It's my favourite meal.'

'That right?'

'Yes, a proper cooked breakfast, bacon, egg, sausage . . .'

'Mushrooms . . .'

'Yes, love mushrooms . . . black pudding.'

'Black pudding? Didn't figure you for a black pudding type, petal, thought you were a bit posh, thought only the ordinary people like me ate black pudding.'

'Oh, you'd be surprised.' She risked eye contact and smiled an approving smile. Intuitively she felt she had to keep him as Horace for as long as she could and the best way she felt she could do that was to encourage him to like being 'Horace'. She smiled a warm smile. 'Tomatoes

170

. . . fried bread, everything that's bad for you . . . and that includes black pudding.'

'Aye . . . clogs your arteries, but once a week.'

'Once a week can't harm.' So it was Sunday . . . Sunday, Sunday, Sunday. 'And even posh folk eat black pudding.'

'Tony likes a good breakfast. Did it for Tony, really, and the pork. You like roast pork?'

'Love it.'

The man paused. 'It's not three bad. We're having it later today . . . me and Tony . . . it's Tony's favourite meat. Tony wants it today, so we're having it.'

'I see . . . so Tony gets what Tony wants?'

'Yes.'

'You must like Tony?'

'Like? I don't know about like. Tony can be a bad lad, a proper bad lad. You don't want to get on the wrong side of Tony.'

'No?'

'No. I don't . . . I'm frightened of Tony, see. Don't like what he does . . . Those people out there . . . every tree is a dead person. Then there was that lassie in Holgate, and last night that old guy, then there's you. Tony's killing you.'

Linda Handy paused as, yet again, a chill shot down her spine. The calmness, the matter-of-factness . . . These are human lives 'Horace' is talking about, one being hers. It was all horribly real, but with a strange sense that it all wasn't happening mixed into the pottage.

'Do you like what Tony's doing, Horace?'

'No. Just told you. It's bad . . . bad . . .'

'You don't have to go along with it, Horace.' She kept her voice soft, warm, motherly.

'I do. Tony . . . he's in control . . . he controls all things but I wish we could stop . . . but Tony won't . . . Wrote that yesterday after Tony had done in the old guy. When

171

Tony wasn't looking, I wrote on the wall of the old guy's room, I wrote for them to please stop us.'

'So you know what's right, don't you, Horace?'

'Yes . . . but Tony.' The man paused. 'Do you have any kids?'

'Three.'

'You must be a good mum, I like talking to you. I can talk to you when Tony isn't here.'

'Where is he now?'

'Don't know . . . don't know where he goes, but he knows where I am.'

'Can I talk to Tony?' It was a gamble to summon the demon but Linda Handy thought it a gamble worth taking.

The man paused. He seemed to stare into the middle distance. His head drew back as if from an unpleasant smell. Then he said, 'No, no, you can't. He's not here. There's just the two of us.'

That was interesting. Tony is quite deeply buried. Can't be summoned at will. It would be more dangerous if he was near the surface.

'I like talking to you,' the man smiled. 'I never had a mother, not like the ones you see on TV or the ones who take their kids to school.'

'You don't have good memories of your own mother or father?'

'No. Me and Tony grew up in Sheffield.'

'You go back a long way then?'

'Schooldays. Tony always was the wild one. Always in trouble, always getting up to badness . . . wrecking things. I never did anything like that, but Tony did.'

'I see.'

'But Tony's not all bad . . . You know the people out there . . .' The man nodded towards the window, through which an unseasonal shaft of sunlight shone. 'Those people, they're all women, except one, eleven women . . .

one man. Tony had it in for the guy . . . don't know why
. . . something personal but it doesn't take much to set
Tony off, a look will do it. But women, Tony never did
anything to them when they were dying, getting hungrier
and weaker and hungrier and weaker. Never did nothing
to them all the time . . . never let me do anything either,
made sure they had enough to drink and emptied the
bucket once a day and when it was near the end, when
they were so far gone they could hardly stand, he'd unchain
them and take them outside and show them the nice pit
he'd dug for them, show them where they were going and
he showed them the apple tree sapling he'd bought to plant
over them. He did that at night though . . . in case they
were seen.'

So this building is not so remote that it can't be overlooked. Linda Handy was learning a little more each time
she met the man, be he 'Horace' or be he 'Tony'.

Then she asked, 'Is there just you and Tony?'

The man looked at her. 'There's Davy. He's here, good
old Davy, he was always there for us. He was always there
for me and Tony, Davy was. Davy's a good lad. Me and
Tony won't ever let nothing happen to Davy.'

'I'd like to talk to David . . . or Davy . . . as you call
him.'

The man sat forward as a change seemed to cross his
eyes. 'Yes?'

'David?'

'Yes.' 'David' seemed nervous, shy almost.

'Nice to meet you.'

He smiled nervously. He fidgeted in his seat.

'Do you like what Horace and Tony are doing?'

He shrugged. The woman thought he didn't know what
to say. She thought his mannerisms were that of a fifteen-
year-old, a classic 'keeper of the pain' who never ages,
which would make the man about ten or twelve when

173

whatever dreadful 'it' had happened or had begun and which had produced 'Horace' and 'Tony'.

'Davy doesn't come out much.' It was clearly 'Horace' again. 'It means he likes you.'

The woman smiled. 'I liked him . . . he seemed to be a nice boy.'

'You think so?'

'Yes . . . didn't get to chat to him much. Do you think I can talk to him again?'

'Tony won't like it. Tony doesn't like me or Davy talking to anyone. *Shut up!* You . . .' The voice became hard, menacing. Tony had returned . . . had awoken. 'You don't talk to Horace . . . see . . . and you don't talk to Davy, especially not Davy . . . not ever Davy.'

She averted her gaze, kept her eyes downcast, focused on the floor as an uneaten piece of bacon was tossed to her. She snatched it up. 'That's to make it worse for you, not better. Understand!'

'Yes,' she said, meekly submissive. Tony had to be acquiesced to. Horace could be mothered, and Tony had to be humoured. But she was still learning. While she was alive, she was learning and while she was alive, there was hope. The building she was in was evidently not at all as remote as she had feared. She was cultivating a relationship with one of her abductor's personalities. There was indeed hope.

'I hope you hadn't planned anything today, ma'am?'

Louise D'Acre threw George Hennessey a pained look as if to say: You should know better.

Hennessey, receptive to the look, said, 'Sorry, silly of me.'

'Well, it has a form of compensation.' Dr D'Acre surveyed the corpse of Martin Welsh. 'My daughters and I were intending to spend the day at the stables . . . sharing our horse. This way they get him between them, more riding time for them, none for me, but more for them. Confess they could hardly contain their glee when I told them I had to work instead of going to the stables. Well, the deceased is a frail, elderly male who seems to be in a good state of nourishment.' Dr D'Acre spoke for the benefit of the microphone which was attached to the end of an anglepoise arm affixed to the ceiling of the pathology laboratory of the York District Hospital. George Hennessey, observing for the police, stood against the wall. Eric Filey, the mortuary assistant, stood closer to the table, ready and willing to be of whatever assistance was required of him by Dr D'Acre. All three persons were dressed in identical, disposable green coveralls. Hennessey watched Filey. He liked the man, finding him jovial and warm and eager. It was very unusual, in Hennessey's experience, to find a man whose personality would seem to lend itself to working with the living choosing, rather, to work with the dead.

It was, in the event, a rapidly concluded post-mortem. Not unprofessionally rapid. It was thorough and with painstaking attention to detail but was not complicated by contrary indications, thus enabling Dr D'Acre to turn to Hennessey one hour after commencing the examination and say, 'Asphyxia, that is the cause of death.'

'I see.'

'There's no indication of any other cause of death, and the small pinpricks in the eyes, which we call petechial haemorrhages . . . they are also on his face . . . are indications, though not absolute proof, of mechanical asphyxia . . . specifically suffocation in this case . . . found with the plastic bag over his head . . . No other injuries . . . well nourished . . . it was the plastic bag that did it.'

'Time of death?'

Dr D'Acre smiled. 'I knew you'd ask that. A matter of

hours before he was found, the flat was warm, the temperature was well turned up. The room temperature and the rectal temperature I took at that time would indicate a time of about twelve to eighteen hours before he was found . . . that sort of timescale.'

'Well, thanks.' Hennessey smiled. 'Thank you for doing this for us. I hope you can rescue something of the day.'

'You know, I might just do that.' She smiled to herself. 'Finish here, scrub off . . . I could grab a bite in the canteen, they'll still be serving . . . drive back out to Skelton, turn up at the stables. Yes, that will put my daughters' noses well out of joint, having to share the horse with me after all . . . and they can't complain . . . it's my animal, not a family pet and I pay all the fees. Yes, thank you, Chief Inspector, thank you for putting that notion in my mind. I will definitely be able to rescue something of the day, after all.'

Hennessey and Yellich sat in Hennessey's office. Both had partaken of lunch, Hennessey at Ye Olde Starre Inn on Sandgate, where his favourite meal of Cumberland sausage with thick onion gravy had gone down very well, especially as he was able to occupy his favourite seat in the corner under low beams with the framed facsimile of a map of 'Yorkshyre' dated 1610 hanging on the wall behind him. Somerled Yellich, pleading a tight budget, had eaten in the generously subsidized police canteen. After eating, they had an agreed rendezvous in the Chief Inspector's office.

'Twelve murders,' he broke the silence. 'Sandra Tupper and Martin Welsh make fourteen.'

'And unless we get a break soon, Linda Handy, of this parish, will make fifteen.' Yellich sipped his tea. 'That's quite a tally.'

'The press will be baying for blood as well. Why were

176

the disappearances not linked? I can see the headlines and the Chief Constable will want his answers from Commander Sharkey and he'll want his answers from me. There will be a "far-reaching inquiry". Is that the phrase normally used?'

'It rings bells, boss,' Yellich smiled. 'I've heard it before somewhere.'

There was another period of silence, broken when Hennessey said, 'Thought I might have seen Charles this weekend.'

'Your son, skipper?'

'Yes . . . but I know he's got a huge case at Teeside Crown Court . . . immensely complicated . . . tax evasion on a massive scale. He's for the Crown and his biggest problem is to put the prosecution case across in a way in which the jury can understand it . . . and quite difficult when the juries are often not composed of the brightest buttons in the box.'

'Yes.' Yellich cradled his mug of tea. 'The people most needed on juries have a means of avoiding jury service. I once heard of a piece of graffiti in the cells of the Old Bailey: "Are twelve people who are so stupid that they can't avoid writing off a few months of their lives really up to deciding whether I should be robbed of several years of mine"?'

Hennessey laughed.

'Probably apocryphal.' Yellich continued, 'It's highly unlikely that any convicted person in the cells or the Old Bailey or any other court would have access to a pen or pencil.'

'Yes . . . weapon or instrument of self harm, but the point is made, the professional people we need on juries have a means of avoiding service. I despair sometimes when I watch a jury during a trial, people who are clearly not focusing . . . the young woman abstractedly filing her

177

nails. It is the case, I think, that one or two people actually form a jury and sway the other ten or eleven during the deliberation.' He paused as a sharp knock came upon his door. 'Yes, come in.'

'Sorry for the delay, sir –' the police artist entered the room – 'but when I told that lady to take her time, she took me at my word. Anyway, this is the CD-fit you requested.' He handed it to Hennessey and withdrew.

Hennessey looked at the CD-fit. 'Heavens, Mr Anybody and Mr Very Ordinary . . . a face in a bus queue, but it might jog someone's memory.' He handed the CD-fit to Yellich.

'Heavens!' Yellich put his mug down on Hennessey's desk. 'It's not Mr Anybody, boss. I knew I'd seen that guy on the CCTV footage.'

'You recognize him?'

'Yes.' Yellich smiled. 'And my idea about following up the Whitelands bag was right all along.'

'It was?'

'Yes . . . it took us right to him, except we didn't realize it.'

'So, who is it?'

'Thornton . . . don't know his first name . . . he runs the World Beer Centre in Holgate. It's him, I tell you, it's him.'

'He's not here.' Mrs Thornton was slender, softly spoken and, even when casually dressed in pastel shades, was clearly a rich man's wife. 'He's in Sheffield. Doubt if he'd help you anyway, you'd have to force him to give you information, charge him with obstruction. I am Moira . . . his wife.'

'We could do that,' Hennessey growled.

Mrs Thornton smiled. She stood in the doorway of Tewkesbury Hall, framed by solid stone. 'You mustn't take his dislike of the police personally, it goes back a long way. His father wore the old blue uniform and each time he came home from policing Sheffield with his truncheon, he started to police his family, also with his truncheon.'

'I am sorry to hear that.'

'It explains Stanley's attitude, but he's really more angry for his mother and younger brother, they are the ones that got it worst. The middle brother escaped into the Army, the father liked Stanley for some reason, but for some other reason, he just had it in for Horace and when his mother tried to protect him . . . well, so Stanley said. Only have his word for it, his mother died before I met Stanley and the father –' she shrugged – 'well, he disappeared.'

'Disappeared?'

'So they said . . . just didn't come home from work one day, one two till ten turn. Was seen to leave the station just after eleven p.m. that night . . . he was a widower by then . . . and didn't come home, so his sons said. Big search for him, serving police officer and all.'

'There would be.'

'Never found his body.'

'What do you think happened?'

'Horace.' She smiled a knowing smile. 'There was only Stanley and Horace at home at the time . . . Norman was in Cyprus.'

'You're implying the two brothers cooked something up?'

'I'm not imply anything . . . but patricide is not unknown and if you have enough time, you can dispose of a body in such a way that it will never be found. What do you want to see my husband about, anyway?'

'We need to trace Horace. He's not at the World Beer Centre he runs.'

'He wouldn't be . . . doesn't open during the day, only

after six p.m. and never on Sunday. He'll be at his house.
You could try there.'
  'What is his address?'
  'You didn't get it from me, OK?'
  'Agreed.'

'Now what?' Yellich appealed to Hennessey.
  'We wait . . . it's all we can do . . . he'll surface at some
time.'
  Yellich, Hennessey, a sergeant and three constables had
converged on the address given by Moira Thornton. There
was no answer to the door, not a sound from inside.
Hennessey had said, 'Punt it in,' and the door was 'punted
in' by the shoulders of two constables. Inside the small
bungalow, which was on the edge of the village of Barton
le Willows, the officers found evidence of only one person
living there – one bed, the washing of one meal, one
person's clothing – but yet, somewhat curiously, a length
of chain attached to the skirting board, an open padlock
and a plastic bucket containing a little human waste. It
was upon finding the bungalow empty that Yellich had
said, 'Now what?'
  'Better put alerts out as well to all mobiles and foot
patrols . . . he's believed to be driving a white van, his
CD-fit will have been circulated by now.'
  'Yes, sir.' Yellich reached into his pocket for his mobile.
Before he could send, it rang. He answered it. 'DS Yellich
. . .' And Hennessey watched his mouth fall open as he
listened. 'Right . . . get a car right there, nearest unit, then
put her through.' He handed his mobile to Hennessey. 'Know
you hate brain-fryers, sir, but I think you'll want this call.'
  'Oh?' Hennessey took the phone and held it to his ear.
'Who is it?'
  'A lady called Handy, wants to speak to the officer in
charge of the investigation into her abduction.'

Thirty minutes later Hennessey and Yellich and two of the constables rendezvoused with Linda Handy. It was a remote location, by a telephone kiosk on a 'B' road, flat fields around with a scattering of roof tops in the distance on all points of the compass. A small wood broke up the flat landscape. Horace Thornton sat in the rear of the police car which, being the nearest unit at the time of the phone call, had arrived and seized control of the situation. Hennessey thought Horace Thornton to look calm, relaxed, pleased almost, but he was definitely the man depicted in the CD-fit depicted by Mrs Haden, warden of Clouston Court. Linda Handy leaned against Yellich's car eating ravenously of a packed meal of sandwiches. It was, she explained, one of the constable's lunches. She was also, she explained, unharmed 'but a trifle peckish'.

'How did you escape?'

'In the end I appealed to Horace's need to look after Davy.'

'There's more than one person?' Hennessey gasped. 'So we are dealing with a gang? Where are the others . . . ? You'll have to give us a description.'

Linda Handy swallowed a mouthful of ham sandwich and said, 'Don't worry, he's all there is . . . just one person . . . just him . . . but three personalities that I can detect. There's "Horace", there's "Tony" and there's "Davy". Davy is about fifteen and was an older brother to Horace when whatever awfulness in their home happened, but as is always the case, as Horace grew older "Davy" remained fifteen years old. "Tony" is the bad one . . . and Horace is in conflict with "Tony". Horace doesn't like what "Tony" is doing but is afraid of him. Began to talk to Horace, gave him the approval he doesn't seem to have had in his life. I told him he owed a duty to "Davy", he had to protect "Davy" from "Tony". That did the trick . . . he rescued me from "Tony" to save "Davy" from "Tony". We got out of the house and drove away together, just drove, quite calmly, though I was with a butterfly stomach.'

'I'll bet.'

'We saw the phone box and without prompting, Horace said, "Time to stop . . . time to stop . . ." and waited while I dialled the three nines . . . and here you are.'

'You sound like you knew what you were doing.'

'Never want to do it again. I'm a forensic psychologist, I put some theory into practice . . . but it's not an experience I want to repeat. The longer I kept Horace on the surface, the more I made life comfortable for him, the less chance there was of "Tony" surfacing, though ironically it was "Tony" who gave me a little food.' Linda Handy explained what she meant. Then she said, 'This won't come to trial.'

'Unfit to plead by reason of insanity, you mean?' A gust of wind tugged at Hennessey's collar.

'Yes . . . a very, very long, perhaps lifelong, stay in a secure hospital. You see, if he is to be believed, between him and "Tony" they have killed quite a number of people. You might like to check underneath the apple trees in his front garden. He told me that he buries the bones of his victims after he had chopped up the body, and plants an apple tree over them.'

'The apple trees,' Hennessey echoed.

'Tell me,' Hennessey asked, as the clock in the large kitchen chimed ten p.m., 'what does the word "eclectic" mean?'

'"Eclectic"?' The woman mused. 'Nice word . . . very punchy . . . I can look it up.'

'Don't go to any trouble, I can look it up just as easily.'

'Well, I think it means "subscribing to more than one philosophy". Why do you ask?'

'Just that early in the week a man described his mind

as "eclectic" . . . went on to say it makes him good at Trivial Pursuits. I think he meant he could absorb much diverse information from various sources.'

'Which is indeed another definition, so I believe. I know the sort of mind he claims to have.' Louise D'Acre smiled and reached across and took Hennessey's hand. 'It's gone quiet upstairs, shall we go up?'